BITTERROOT VALLEY

BOOK ONE OF THE SERIES

FOLLOWING ON

WHITE HORSES

JACK & JUDY BONHAM

TOUCH
PUBLISHING

Following on White Horses
Book One: Bitterroot Valley
Copyright © 2016 Jack and Judy Bonham

ISBN: 978-1-942508-29-8

Published by Touch Publishing
P.O. Box 180303
Arlington, Texas 76096 U.S.A.
www.TouchPublishingServices.com

Library of Congress Control Number: 2016946419

Contact the author:
www.BitterrootValleyBook.com

Dedication

To our covenant with horses.

They brought the doctor who delivered the babies. They taught our children responsibility. They took us to work, to war, brought us home to the peace and in the end delivered us to the grave.

We have a covenant and the horses have not forgotten.

For Hershey
Quarter Horse / 100% Heart
Our Beautiful Mare
Every one of her steps brought her closer to our hearts.
2002-2016

And the armies which were in heaven followed him upon white horses, clothed in fine linen, white and clean.
Revelation 19:14

PROLOGUE

Cheyenne Memorial Hospital

I've had such an interesting life, I wish it could continue. But I'm old, and it doesn't look like I'll be getting back to my ranch before this life has ended. As such, I've called my granddaughter to come to the hospital. Don't worry, she's not a kid. Well, I guess compared to me she is, but she's old enough to hear what I have to tell her. She knows some of these things. Some will surprise her. Her grandmother and I always thought there were certain parts of the family tree that required her maturity before they could be understood. Ready or not, the time is now.

She'll be here any minute. It's funny, but I almost wish she wasn't coming. Almost. I dread the reliving of the past. In my honesty with her, I have to return to the pain of my childhood, and there will be tears, make no doubt about it. Grief. Loss. It must happen. No matter how I appear to those around me, this crusty old man still has a softness in my heart when it comes to life and the people I have loved.

I wish Cheyenne were here. She would know exactly how to tell this awkward story and I could lean back and listen and watch my granddaughter's eyes for reaction. That wouldn't keep me from crying though, you understand. Cheyenne passed away exactly twelve years, nine months, and twenty-five days ago. Not that I'm counting the time. I miss her, let's just leave it at that.

Mariah, our granddaughter, is beautiful in an exotic sort of way. I don't just say that because I see a bit of my wife in her, and myself too, I suppose, but I know she's beautiful through and through. Her spirit mirrors that of her grandmother and I often catch glimpses of another woman in her, one I may tell you about later.

I'm recording this introduction to my story on a little digital recorder Mariah gave me a few weeks back. I think she thought it would prolong my life. Maybe I did too. But I let it sit on the bedside table long enough. I'm not so stupid as to think talking into this machine will give me more days than I've got, even if I can't figure out how this contraption that is smaller than my thumb is keeping track of my words. Mariah thinks she's coming here to pick the recorder up. I guess she figures she'll take it home and listen when she has the time.

But I don't want this to be a one-way street. I don't want her to sit down *someday* and listen to what ol' Gramps had to say. I'll record it all right, but I'll do so while I look into her eyes. The living, expressive face of someone I dearly love. There are two reasons for this. One, if I'm not looking at her, I might have a tendency to lie. Historically I've lived by Twain's adage: "There's no reason to mess up a good story by sticking to the facts." Talking directly to her will keep that 3-inch fish from becoming a 30-inch whopper.

In any case, some of it won't be on the money because all of this happened a long time ago, and there's bound to be a discrepancy between what I remember and what I'll tell. Although, I have to say, in the last few years the past has lighted up inside my brain like a movie which is ready to be played again. I hope this doesn't mean I'm about to get senile, or whatever they're calling it nowadays, but it probably does.

That's the second reason I need to speak this aloud to Mariah. She's got eyes like her grandma and those eyes will keep me on track as I endeavor to tell my tale.

I hear a commotion outside, and that's probably her now. I sure hope she doesn't have any plans for the next few hours. Oh well. If she does, I've always got the stupid machine to rely upon.

"Hey, darlin'," I say as she enters the room.

"Hey, Gramps." She strides over to the bed and not only hugs me, but gives me a big kiss on the mouth. Sure hope I remembered to brush my teeth this morning. I try not to breathe right in her face.

She glances at the little recorder and notices that the light is on.

"You just finishing up?"

"I wish."

"Need a few moments alone, do you?"

"Hell no," I say. "I've had enough of being alone to last the rest of my life." This makes her smile.

"So, did you finish the story?"

"Sit down darlin', I've got something to tell you."

She pulls the straight-backed plastic chair over to the bed.

"No, you'd better pull that lounge chair over, this may take a while."

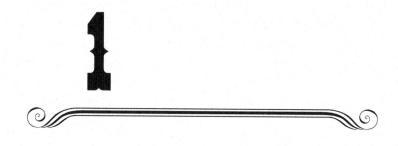

1

The wind blew hard from the south. Not in gusts—it was a steady forty mile an hour pusher. The flag outside of the white clapboard church was looking a lot like the flag Neil Armstrong planted on the moon, except if you listened you could actually hear this one tearing at the seams in the stars, threatening the hem of it all.

Snap...Snap...Snap

An early harvest moon had risen in the east and it, too, seemed to be blown by the wind. The thick clouds gave the illusion of standing still as the moon raced across the windblown sky.

I'd noticed all of this before I'd gone into the tiny church and even from inside I could tell it was still blowing strongly.

As I was being dragged along the worn church carpet by a man in his seventies, I wondered how the flag was holding up. The oddity of my wondering such a thing wasn't lost on me. He kicked the door open and the wind caught it, pressing it back against the front of the church, straining the old brass hinges till the screws groaned in the door frame.

I tried to break free as the silver-haired gentle-man fruitlessly pulled one-handed at the open door to close it.

Flap...flap...flap went the door. It made a nice accompaniment to the *snap...snap...snapping* of the flag.

Another man leaned out from the church and yanked the door closed with a slam; the punctuation on my eviction. The older man with the silver comb-over grabbed both my arms and drug me over to the traffic circle in front of the church.

In the middle of the dirt circle was a raised area that housed a picnic table and some shade trees. He took me over to the table. If you'd been standing out there, at first it would have seemed as if I was crying, but by now it would have been obvious the sound coming from my mouth was laughter. Tears rolled down my ten-year-old face—the tears which laughter can sometimes make. The older man had had enough.

"Sit! Sit down!"

I sat and tried hard to catch the breath which had been stolen by my laughter.

"And stop that god-damned laughing!" he commanded.

"But you don't understand—" I started to say.

"I sure as hell do understand. I understand that while viewing the open caskets of your mother and father you broke out in laughter. There ain't nothin' funny about your folks losin' their lives in the middle of their prime in some stupid car accident!"

"Did you see their faces?" I asked.

I didn't see his fist coming until it met with my jaw. It probably wasn't what he intended to do, but it was done, and by the time I hit the ground I was out cold. Well, at least that's what the man thought. I had momentarily lost consciousness, then came back pretty quickly. I was smart enough to keep my eyes closed, not wishing to taste his fist again across my mouth.

From inside the church I could hear the preacher warn: "This is the way it happened, like a thief in the night. There's no hill on which the old wait patiently to die and the young go down the same hill waiting without caring because they know it is not their time."

It was hard to keep my eyes closed as he hoisted me over his shoulder and carried me like a carcass of meat back into the church. As the church door whammed open once again, those asleep, or nearly so, were brought back into the land of the living and those awake had their hearts jump within their chests.

5

Everyone turned toward the sound and probably the same man who had shut the door previously got up and did so again.

No one peeped as comb-over man carried my supposedly unconscious body to the front of the church and laid me on the altar. The preacher, never one to squander a moment of drama, immediately changed gears.

"It was our father Abraham who took his only son, Isaac, up on Mount Mortimer and tying him up, laid his body on the altar. God had wanted to test Abraham's faith so he'd told the old man to give up the one thing which made him and Sara a family, their only born son, their child of laughter. And today we have witnessed God's acquisition of these two young parents questioning whether their young son would be willing to let go of what went to make up what he considered family.

"Thank you, brother Snook," the preacher said to the old man. I snuck a peek and could see him running his fingers through what remained of his hair as he returned to his seat.

"Brother Snook has brought to the altar the unconscious body of a young boy lost in the middle of his loss." The preacher placed one of his gnarled hands on my cool forehead. His hand was burning hot. "In answer to God's question, this young man, like the mother of Isaac when told she would bear a child in her old age, this young man's answer was the same as hers—laughter! Let us not be too harsh on this boy, John Wilson Barnes, for how many of us at such a tender age is asked such a tough question?"

As the preacher asked everyone to join him in prayer, and they all squeezed their eyes shut, I sat up on the altar. I wasn't sure where all this was leading, but I certainly didn't believe there would be another ram stuck in the brambles.

I looked out upon the community of faith where me and my parents had taken Holy Communion every Sunday. I looked out upon the bowed heads and the closed eyes of those who had sworn a holy covenant to raise me in the spirit of Jesus. I looked out and realized there was not one family in that so-called fold

6

who would be willing to feed another mouth, clothe another body, or guide another soul. There was no one there for me except my dead mother and father, and quite frankly I felt—embarrassed. Embarrassed that those of a false covenant should be able to look upon the only two people of a true covenant.

I slipped silently from my perch on the altar and walked to my parents' coffins. I kissed them both on their sewn-shut mouths and inched the coffin lids down slowly. Then I slipped out the back door through the pastor's office.

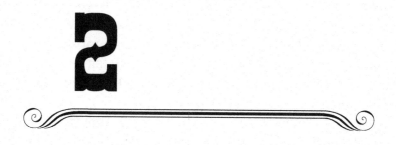

From my hiding spot in the bushes I watched the last of the cars back up and leave the parking lot of the little whitewashed clapboard church. The pastor exited shortly after, giving the front door a hard shove to make sure it closed properly. He turned and walked toward the only pick-up truck left in the parking lot.

There was one other vehicle parked across the lot from the pastor's truck. As the pastor crossed the lot, the driver's side door of that vehicle opened, and a woman in her early fifties got out.

Half-way to his truck the pastor realized this woman of medium build and salt and pepper short cropped hair intended to intercept him. He stopped and turned in her direction without walking toward her.

"Can I help you, ma'am?"

The woman continued with her measured stride until she was barely three feet from where the pastor stood.

"Don't you just love these Bitterroot Valley evenings in the summer?" she asked, gazing toward the Bitterroot's jagged peaks, where the setting sun blasted the evening sky with brilliant yellows, reds, and pinks. These colors were contrasted against a hurtful blue sky which had turned lavender halfway across its dome to the east.

The pastor didn't speak.

"This is my favorite time of year," she said, eyes fixed upon the Bitterroot Mountains.

The pastor still didn't speak.

"I've come for the boy," she said, her eyes now searching the pastor's face for some sort of response.

"He ain't here," was all the pastor said.

"Did he leave with one of your parishioners?"

"He left, that's for sure."

"Where'd he go?" she asked, looking around the parking lot.

"Out the back door during the service."

"You don't have any idea where he is?"

"He ain't here," was all the pastor said.

"He's one of your flock, aren't you concerned?"

"Frankly he's not in his right mind."

"He lost both his parents in a terrible car crash."

"He should have been with them."

"Are you saying he ought to be dead?"

"Better dead than possessed with the mind of a devil."

"Possessed?"

"He laughed at them in their coffins."

"OK."

"He wouldn't stop laughing—"

"Goodness."

"Goodness didn't have nothing to do with it."

"I was hoping one of your flock would take him in until we could find a placement for him."

The pastor didn't reply.

"He's only a boy of ten," she persisted.

"You weren't here; you didn't hear that laughter, see the mocking face."

"Do you have any idea which way he went?"

"The Bitterroot is the same size as the Dead Sea, ten miles wide and fifty miles long."

"And the direction?"

"He's still here," said the pastor as his eyes scanned the darkening fields and the Bitterroot Mountains beyond, "and I'll feel a lot better once he's gone. Good night."

The pastor walked to his pick-up, got in, fired up the old, oil-burning V-8 engine, and scattered gravel which barely missed me as he spun the truck out on the macadam.

The lady watched after the pastor's truck until his red brake lights were no longer visible. At one point she looked right at me, and even though I was sure she saw me, she didn't. Just got in her car, started it up, and drove off.

I walked north on Eastside Highway as far as Hamilton Heights Road. I knew that road well because my father, Zack, had taken me up to Calf Creek at the end of the road and we'd ridden borrowed horses up there. I had no intention of going that far east. I stepped off Hamilton Heights Road where there was a sign that advertised horses, sold and trained. This was the place Dad and I had rented from. I skirted the pasture and after climbing a fence, walked to the barn, whose western facing door was open to the night.

Inside the barn I found two stalls which were being used for storage. The second stall had a child's mattress propped up on its side. I took the mattress down and laid it behind a stack of boxes easily as tall as I was. Then I walked back out and peed into the straw laying on the floor of the barn. Dad and I had done the same thing the day we'd ridden those horses. The rancher didn't care. In fact, he'd told us to go ahead when I said I had to pee.

I was with my mom and dad. It seemed perfectly natural. We were at the grocery store, and my father was pushing the cart and smiling. Mother was talking about the wonderful meals they were going to have in the weeks to come. My mouth was watering: BBQ chicken, rice, and corn on the cob; meatloaf, mashed potatoes and gravy with green peas; marinated top sirloin steak with baked potatoes and a green salad—I started thinking about the snacks and junk foods I loved. I grabbed a twelve pack of Reese's cups and a six pack of Pepsi and put them in the cart.

"Good boy," Dad said and smiled a really winning smile.

Encouraged by my dad's smile, I grabbed a couple of bags of potato chips and some Hostess cupcakes. When I placed them in the cart, I noticed my dad was eating from the open Reese's twelve pack. He was stuffing the Reese's in as fast as he could and chewing like a cow on his cud. Brown juice drooled from the corner of dad's mouth.

Mother came back from the meat counter with a section of butcher paper wrapped meats. When she saw the brown drool on father's face, instead of scolding him, she simply licked the melting chocolate off his face.

I awakened with a start and sat bolt upright on the mattress in the barn. My stomach growled deeply and I realized how very hungry I was. When was the last time I'd eaten? I couldn't honestly remember. I might be only ten years old, but hunger was hunger!

I got up and walked outside the barn. The night was clear as crystal and a multitude of stars covered the dome of the sky. I easily found the Big Dipper—my dad had taught me that one. There was a way to find the Little Dipper by using the Big Dipper, but I couldn't remember how that worked. I wished I could talk to my father and ask him.

Suddenly I knew someone was standing behind me. There hadn't been a sound or anything to give the person away, but I knew just the same that here in the wee hours of the morning I'd been discovered.

I turned slowly. There on the other side of the fence stood a paint horse. He was big, probably sixteen hands at the withers. He snorted a gentle, *"Hello, how are you?"* snort. Immediately I recognized him as the one I'd ridden a couple years before with my dad.

I climbed the fence. The horse remained standing next to it. His only response was to pitch his head back toward his middle as if to say, "Climb aboard, please."

I swung one leg over and we abandoned the fence line. The horse began walking away from the halogen lights surrounding the out buildings and toward the middle of the darkened pasture.

I started to leap off. I wasn't sure I liked the darkened pasture. Too much like the field of graves I'd seen at Riverside Cemetery, on the banks of the Bitterroot River, just West of Hamilton. But as I was about to pull my leg over and jump, the paint took off in a lope. I grabbed his long mane and held on. I knew how to ride. Neighbors had let me ride their horses, and a kindly old vet had given my family a broken down sorrel named Candy Bar. I'd spent nearly an entire summer on Candy Bar before she got the colic and died.

I got into the rhythm of the gentle lope and before I knew it me and the paint were way out into the darkness of the pasture. I could hear the irrigation ditch running deep as the horse came to a halt.

I looked back toward the barn and the lights of the out buildings. They were at least a football field away. I started to get scared again when the paint snorted and pitched his head and nose toward the heavens.

"My! My!" I thought, as what had only been a black sky with hundreds of stars had turned into a sky filled almost beyond belief with stars. There was my favorite candy bar, the Milky Way, next to my old horse. Those stars made a broad swipe of splattered pin pricks splitting the midnight sky with an intensity of what might be!

The horse slowed to a stop and together we stood silently in the inkiness of that pasture with our heads lifted toward the heavens. I remembered a prayer I'd heard everyone say in church, "Our Father—" I spoke out loud.

At that moment the horse whinnied low in his throat.

I started again, "Our Father—" again the paint whinnied low.

It was then I realized me and the horse were in the presence of someone else. I couldn't exactly say how I knew; I think it was the paint who told me. It wasn't like with my dad, it was more like the Father of it all—the Maker of it all, the Creator of it all.

"I think this is the first time I've known you were really here," I said aloud.

I brought my gaze down toward the horizon and in a flash thought I saw, no, I did see it—a kindly man with a white beard down his chest. He was riding a white horse and wearing a robe like the one Jesus was always pictured in, in those church paintings. Then, that image disappeared and I realized there was a cowboy there, saddled up and riding a paint horse like the one I was on.

"Is this your horse?" I asked.

The cowboy nodded his head. I kicked the paint in the ribs and rode toward him.

The cowboy had a wild rag loosely tied about his neck. He wore a plain, white linen shirt with blue ticking on it. It reminded

13

me of my old mattress. His mud-colored pants were held up with a wide belt. I could see his six-shooter cross draw on his left thigh. Brown, dirty boots had big Texas style spurs jingling ever so slightly as he sat there on his horse.

"Look, I'm sorry, the horse sort of invited me up on him," I explained.

"That's a wonderful invitation, wouldn't you say, partner?"

"Yeah. Glad you understand."

"Oh, I do, I do."

"I was praying back there, did you hear me?"

"Is that what you was doing?"

"Yeah. Kinda silly, I know."

"Nothing wrong with praying."

"Really?"

"Absolutely nothing, partner."

I started to get off the horse, but the cowboy warned me with a look I should stay mounted.

"Don't you want your horse back?"

"He's fine with you on him."

"I've ridden him before, ya know?"

"I know."

"But you weren't the rancher Dad and I rented him from."

"I saw ya, nonetheless."

"What are you up and saddled for this early in the morning? Going to push some cows?"

"Goin' on a little ride."

"Can I go with you?"

"Wish you would."

"Well, I will."

"Then, it's settled."

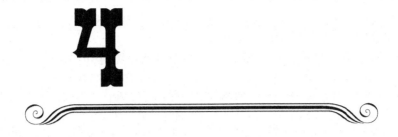

“The man who owns this ranch walks out early.”

"But you know him, right?”

“Like a brother. He’s in his late sixties and there’s joint problems which bother him at night. Bothers him enough that he’ll have to get up and take three aspirin and fill two hot water bottles. They fit nicely around his neck. He don’t sleep well on his back, but usually with the heat he can coax two more hours of sleep out of his old body.”

“Boy, you sure do know him!”

“That I do. He’ll feed the Angus yearling he keeps out front first. He don’t own the yearling, but by feeding and pasturing it he’s able to get half the meat once it’s slaughtered—a lot cheaper than buying the meat.”

“I’ll bet!“

“The only drawback is he’s found the yearling to be playful and at times even entertaining. He leaves a horse bag in that pasture and the yearling always tosses it over the fence. The old man tosses it back in when he feeds, but eventually the red, hard-rubber horse bag ends up outside the pasture again. Once in a while the old man watches from his porch—coffee in hand—but he’s never actually seen the yearling toss the bag over the fence. He’s glad he never saw it. Deep down the old man knows it would make it harder at slaughter time. When he’s done finished with the yearling, next he’ll feed the horses. He’s bound to notice the paint is missing.”

“What should we do?”

"Follow me," said the cowboy, and we started riding hard toward the southernmost fence.

We saw the old man as he stood at the point in the fence where it looked like we'd jump. He could have come over to the fence and taken off his cowboy hat and waved it to scare off the horse, but all the old man did was stand there and watch the two of us, me and the cowboy, coming hell bent for leather toward the fence.

Me and the paint were like one body, one thing, and all the old man did was bring his right hand to the front of his cowboy hat as we sailed over the fence not twelve feet from where he stood.

I made eye-contact with him and saluted back, my other hand wrapped tightly around a tuft of mane. Well, I don't think the old rancher was waving or saluting, my best guess was he was trying to keep the sun out of his eyes to better see us.

As we rode off toward the Sapphire Mountains, the old man ran back into the ranch house. I imagine he was calling the police.

We rode the left side of the road facing traffic on our way up to Calf Creek. It was probably a good three miles up there and just about the same time we saw the parking lot we heard the wail of the sheriff's deputy's car.

As fate would have it, the cruiser and my paint made the parking lot at nearly the same time. The cruiser gunned past and slid sideways blocking the entrance to the riding trails.

Me and the paint never missed a stride. The deputy sheriff got out of the car, pulled his revolver, and fired a warning shot into the air. From a distance, I suppose, it looked as if the gunshot had propelled the paint and I skyward. We cleared the right front quarter panel, but the paint's back hooves came down hard leaving some pretty nifty tracks on the left rear.

"Shit!" yelled the deputy as he aimed the pistol at the cowboy and me. He cocked the pistol, then he must have thought better of it.

"God damn!" he shouted as he uncocked his piece and jammed it back into his holster. I could see the deputy lean into his cruiser, keying his mike.

I couldn't hear what he was saying what with the thundering hooves and all, but I think he was calling for back up. That's what the police usually do.

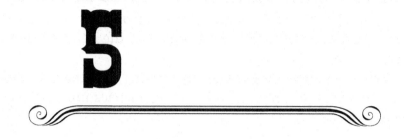

I was doing fine except for the hunger, which was getting me good. If I could have eaten the meadow grasses and weeds like my faithful paint horse I never would have been caught. But the hunger got me. I figured maybe the cowboy had something on him, and we could stop and have a cold breakfast, maybe some jerked meat or something, but when I went to looking for him, he was nowhere to be seen. I thought that was strange, but figured he'd appeared without warning and guessed it was his right to disappear in the same manner. The thought of that jerked meat made my stomach grumble and my mouth water, though.

I spent the first day going high into the Sapphires—way beyond the benches—past the few front ranges. The horse ate when we stopped to rest, and we both drank from the high mountain streams. Water was no problem. Heck, if I could have lived on water alone, I could have made it.

As the sun was sinking behind the Bitterroots, I found a tall cave that went back about fifty feet or so. The horse wouldn't be ridden into the cave, but after a bit of coaxing, or maybe it was the rain which had started up late, the horse finally followed me inside. It was cozy at first. The sun broke through the rain clouds and threw some oranges and reds all the way to the back of the cave. That gave me the opportunity to see it wasn't, nor had it been, a cave used by any bear. It was clear as a whistle, and I built a small fire way in the back and got my own light going before the sun was totally gone. You may wonder how I did that, but hey, I was a ten year old boy and when possible I always carried matches. I'd gathered enough wood to keep the fire going most of the night, and I wasn't worried about no posse, cause there was a bunch of trees right outside the entrance to the cave and they broke up the smoke and kept anyone down below from seeing the fire.

I barely slept that first night even though I loved to sleep to the sound of the rain. Every time I fell asleep I dreamed of Mom's blueberry pancakes dripping with lots of melted butter and one hundred percent real maple syrup. I'd plunge my fork into the pancakes, cut myself off a generous bite, and the minute the sweet smelling cakes would make it to my mouth, I'd wake up. I kept thinking if only I could eat in my dream, maybe I wouldn't be hungry when I woke up.

I tried to go back to sleep, but the smell of sausage and pancakes were in the very air of the cave itself. It seemed a shame I couldn't even eat in my dreams.

I wanted to talk to the cowboy, but for some reason it didn't seem the same without being on my horse. I could imagine the cowboy being there, but without really being there, how could the cowboy be a comfort to me? I imagined I could talk to the cowboy anyway, but that was simply crazy. Nevertheless, I gave it a try.

"I know you're not here with me, but it's weird, somehow I feel you are."

I looked toward the mouth of the cave half expecting to see the cowboy standing there, sort of smiling and sort of not, with his gun on his left hip. But it was only the shadows thrown by the fire.

"We kinda got ourselves into a mess, didn't we? Although, you won't come to no harm cause I don't think they'll catch you. Now me, well, I ain't ever got away with anything. Mom used to tell me whenever I did something wrong I should immediately come and tell her since she was gonna find out any way."

The thought of my mom and dad brought a bunch of tears to my eyes and heck, there was nobody there, and so I laid my head down in my arms and let her rip. The horse moved around uneasily, maybe he'd never heard anybody cry before. Whatever. Eventually, the paint came over and nudged me with his soft nose, and that made me laugh. The laugh startled the horse more than the crying, and he backed up a bit and snorted loudly.

"It's OK, fella, I'm OK. Don't you worry, by tomorrow we'll be fine."

Don't know why I said that, but the moment it was said, I believed it, and that's a fact.

By first light the paint and I were making our way up a swale when the smell of bacon cooking caught both our noses. Blindly following the aroma up the small valley, we found ourselves in the middle of a sheep herd. The horse wouldn't go forward at first, maybe he'd never seen sheep, but that was sort of hard to believe. After he set his ears back and forth a couple of times and sniffed the air real good he moved slowly through the herd. We saw the sheep herder's tent before we saw the sheep herder.

It was hard to tell how old the man was. His beard was all salt and pepper like his long hair, but the body which supported that wizened head belonged to a much younger man.

He squatted over the fire pit, his fork turning bacon slices one after another.

"Well just don't sit there on that fine looking horse, get down and share some breakfast with me," the herder said without looking up. The man's voice was like honey; sweet and substantial.

The herder poured a cup of coffee and set it on the other side of the fire pit.

"I hope you like it black. Sugar attracts ants and milk always goes bad," he said.

I dismounted and the paint began in on the rich meadow grass.

"There's a bar of soap by the tent and the streams—well, follow your ears. Clean-up before you eat."

I said nothing. What was there to say? It looked like he had been expecting me all along. Why was there so much bacon in that pan? Had he planned on eating a pound of bacon all by himself? I took the bar of soap and walked toward the sound of the brook.

"Coffee'll be just right when you get back."

The coffee was just right and it felt good to wash my hands in the stream. It was almost like I was home —washed up and ready for breakfast. Except the sheep herder didn't bother to look at my hands and he hadn't checked behind my ears to see if they were clean.

"Do you like coffee?" the herder asked.

"It tastes like the bass notes on my mother's piano."

"So your mother's a musician, how wonderful."

I said nothing.

"How many eggs do you want?" asked the herder as he flung a dreg of coffee into the fire. The fire sputtered loudly.

"How many do you have?" I really wanted to know.

"I like a man with an appetite," the herder said as he cracked a half a dozen eggs into the hot grease and stirred them vigorously.

The breakfast which the herder served me that particular morning was as good as any breakfast my mother had ever served. Or maybe it was because I was so hungry. I wanted seconds—even after eating my share of the half dozen scrambled eggs, two Dutch oven biscuits, and six slices of bacon. Surprisingly, the coffee tasted best when I was washing my breakfast down.

"That's a good lookin' horse you got there," said the herder.

"Thanks."

"Do you always ride bareback?"

"When I don't have a saddle."

"You make a lot of sense boy."

I said nothing to that.

"I'm fixin' to take this herd higher in the mountains. Me and Johnny-boy could sure use some help."

I looked over at the herder's dog. An Australian sheep dog sat so close to the herder that it looked as if both of them were leaning on each other. Maybe they were. The dog looked at the herder and his face lit up.

"Is that Johnny-boy?"

"Sure is. I'm Conrad."

"I'm John."

"Nice to meet you, John."

"Same here."

"What's a polite boy like you doing up here in the mountains?"

I looked down at the earth between his crossed legs.

"Sorry, I don't much like questions, myself."

"You done asked two."

"I have, haven't I? Well, I'm sorry twice over."

"I can."

"You can?"

"Help with the herd."

"Oh, yeah, OK."

"There'd be six of us, if my friend would show up. That'd be plenty to get them up higher."

"What friend is that?" the herder asked as he began looking round about.

"Oh, just this cowboy I met."

"Sure could use the help, you think he might be around later?"

"Never can tell. He showed up without much fanfare the first time."

"What's his name?"

"He ain't told me yet."

"He got a horse?"

"A beaute!"

"Figures. Wish I had a horse, though most herders wouldn't use one, but I would if I had one."

The herd moved its way easy up the last draw which led to

the upper meadows. Me and the horse were as one as we switched back and forth pushing the stragglers and strays back into the cottony mass of bleating sheep. Johnny-boy and Conrad worked the western slope and all in all it took us less than seven hours to move about fifteen miles.

Strangely, it seemed as if the cowboy was going to appear around the next bend or the next tree. I kept expecting to see him even though I hadn't since yesterday morning.

I spent most of that summer with the sheep herder Conrad and his dog, Johnny-boy. I nearly always felt the presence of the cowboy riding his magnificent horse, smiling graciously, and being the light and strength I needed now that my parents were gone. You'd have thought I'd have given up on that cowboy, but some people make such an impression it's hard to let their feeling go.

Naturally, I thanked Conrad and Johnny-boy every day for everything they were doing for me. Conrad was like the older uncle I never had and I began to think of Johnny-boy more like a brother than a dog.

The herd of sheep grazed generously on the tall meadow grass and as they made their way around the meadow, the grass grew back and supported their voracious appetites.

One night I was awakened by the crack of a rifle. I scooted over toward Conrad, who stood tall looking out into the night.

"What is it?"

"Wolf, probably."

"I don't like wolves."

"Neither does Johnny-boy."

The dog leaned toward the direction we were looking, just begging to have Conrad tell him it was OK to chase whatever was out there.

"You ever kill one?"

"I rarely come close, but it makes no sense not to try."

The lamb that had been killed by the wolf had not been

carried away. Conrad roasted it over the open pit and it was enjoyed by all present. Conrad gave thanks to the Father for the meal of lamb. I remembered my mother calling God's Son the Lamb of God. It seemed to me the wolf had been sent to kill the lamb so the three of us could enjoy a late summer treat and I would be reminded of my mother's words.

I think Conrad began to worry about me after I'd been there for two months. He liked my help, but more than anything else he appreciated the company. Maybe it irked him, though, that he was getting dependent on me for the help. Some men want to think they can do everything without any help. I've heard that called a "self-made" man, and maybe Conrad was becoming attached to me, as I was certainly becoming attached to him and Johnny-boy. The thought of not being with Conrad and the dog gave me a hollow feeling in the pit of my stomach. Maybe Conrad and Johnny-boy felt the same way.

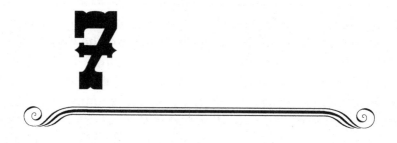

That morning in late summer, that morning which I guessed was toward the middle of September, started out like just about all other mornings that I'd experienced with the sheep herder.

Conrad was up before first light and the smell of coffee and frying bacon wafted its way past the tent flap and into my nose. I lay there that morning trying to remember what it was like having a mother and father. What my life was like before I started living with Uncle Conrad. I had vague memories half frozen in time, half fading away with each new day. Sometimes when I tried to remember my mother's face, I simply couldn't. It was easier to remember my father's face because everyone had always said I was the spitting image of father. If I had trouble remembering father's face all I did was go to the pooled brook and look down at his reflection.

Around the campfire with the light in the east, pink and glowing yellow beneath, I ate my breakfast remembering how hungry I'd been the first day I followed my nose and found the sheep herder.

"I've got to go into town for supplies," Conrad said.

"Will I be here all alone?"

"No, remember, Johnny-boy's here."

"There looks like there's plenty of bacon, plenty of coffee, lots of eggs—"

"I have to go into town that's all there is to it."

"What if a wolf comes when you're gone?"

"You know where I keep the rifle. Take it out, ratchet a round into the chamber like you've seen me do and shoot high. I don't want any of the sheep hit by a stray bullet."

I said nothing to this advice.

"I need to take the horse," he declared.

"My horse?"

"That's the only one in camp. It'll make it easier for me to get into town before it gets dark."

"Can you ride him without a halter or bridle?"

"I have a hackamore."

After the dishes were washed and put away Conrad put the hackamore on the paint. As he rode off I half expected him to turn and wave at some point, but that didn't happen.

The helicopters were there first. I heard them before I saw them. Johnny-boy and I ran to the tree line and hid as a chopper came into view. It swooped down over the five hundred bales of cotton munching on the high green meadows.

I imagined that the herd of sheep, having never seen or heard a helicopter, might have imagined a giant eagle or hawk was swooping down on them to take one or more of them back to its nest. Regardless of what they thought (if sheep do, in fact, think), they scattered this way and that like the Red Sea before Moses.

One half of the herd ran pell-mell over the campsite, knocking down the tent. One unfortunate sheep was rolled through the dying embers of that morning's fire and smoldering, ran like all hell was chasing it. My best guess was since the sheep had never heard of stop, drop, and roll, it just kept running faster fanning the flames as it ran into the dry timber which followed the creek through the meadow.

I stood at the edge of the tree line; the sheep was running right toward me. The creek was behind me, and the sheep might have made it, but its screams were tearing a hole in my brain. I aimed carefully, remembering as my dad had taught me to squeeze the trigger. When the rifle bucked in my arms, the sheep went down, but the flames started a fire in the dry timber. The subsequent smoke covered the sheep herd and sent them running amuck.

I had taken Conrad's rifle from the collapsed tent and yes, I had fired it. Not in the direction of the retreating helicopter as reported, but in the direction of the flaming ewe. I couldn't stand to see an animal suffer and if killing it would end its suffering, then kill it I would.

By the time the four by fours and dozen mounted deputies arrived, the scene was nothing short of a Chinese fire drill.

Evidently, the helicopters had reported a shot fired because all the deputies had their weapons drawn.

A shot had been fired by one of the mounted deputies as a signal, unfortunately prearranged only between those on horseback, that the boy had been spotted.

One of the deputy's horses stepped in a hole and both the horse and deputy went down. They went down with such finality, even I thought someone had shot him.

The sheriff's Jeep roared on the scene, spinning its tires and weaving back and forth through the wet grass, eventually hitting two sheep. I saw them fly through the air and thought about that saying about pigs flying. I wondered what might happen when sheep fly?

We wouldn't have been captured I don't think if we'd have run for it. But Johnny-boy and I felt the sheep were our responsibility, and they were! Johnny-boy was running around the herd bringing them back together and I was running (admittedly with the rifle) trying my best to turn the sheep back into the meadow. As it was Johnny-boy and I—under unbelievably stressful circumstances, in the face of unrelenting danger and without regard to our own safety—managed to pull the herd together upwind of the fire and out of harm's way.

In the world of sheep and sheep herders this easily would have gained each of us—myself and Johnny-boy—a Congressional

Medal of Honor, but under the present circumstances it gained Johnny-boy nothing but a trip to the Ravalli County Pound and me, John Wilson Barnes, a handcuffed trip to the county jail.

That night, sitting in the sheriff's office waiting for Social Services to show up, I saw footage from a local news channel out of Missoula. They'd sent one of their helicopters to the scene and the subsequent footage rivaled any Keystone cops movie I ever saw. It was hard to keep a straight face, and some of the deputies who hadn't been there laughed out loud until the sheriff bawled them out.

For the sheriff to be re-elected in Ravalli County, not to mention the rest of the civilized world, would have been a pretty neat trick. My guess was shutting everybody up the sheriff had decided to eat the whole cow and wasn't about to choke on the tail.

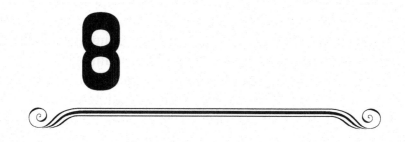

8

In the story of the *Emperor's New Clothes*, it was a small child who spoke the truth concerning a naked, although highly placed, individual, hoodwinked into thinking he was wearing the rarest of materials that had been bonded into garments. An "out of the mouths of babes" revelation enlightened everyone that the Emperor's new clothes were actually the original outfit in which he had arrived here on earth—his birthday suit. This funny realization toppled the ruler from the heights to the depths. A good time was had by all, except, of course, for the naked Emperor.

No such frivolity was forthcoming from the Ravalli County Courthouse the day I, John Wilson Barnes, age 10, stood before the chief magistrate of the court. Indictments were read, stories were told, poor Mr. Conrad testified, and off in the corner a social services worker in the guise of one Miss Ruth Henderson listened to it all. She had no doubt that I would, at this moment, be simply unadoptable. Branded as a child who laughed at his parents' funeral, stole a horse, evaded armed deputies, hung out for two months with a hermit, who may or may not have molested him, and then supposedly shot at the deputies who were trying to rescue him. This would not put confidence in anyone's mind to make them think they could handle such a boy.

The court would not be made fun of, and it was the court's job to see that the law was not only upheld, but held up in the position of respect. The rule of law was the one thing separating humankind from the animals, and it was the court's job to punish those who held it up to ridicule.

Consequently, when Judge Rutherford B. Langston was presented with the police reports and allegations filed against me, he asked if the charges which were read concerning me were accurate.

"Yes sir," I said. "That about covers it, except I think it was wrong Mr. Conrad was arrested and Johnny-boy placed in the Ravalli County Pound."

The judge summed the authorities position all up when he replied, "What you think is not important to this court, son!"

"I'm not your son!" I answered back, to which the judge sagaciously replied, "And for that I am eternally grateful."

I was placed in "respite care"—which meant before the day was out I would be driven from the Ravalli County Jail to a "respite" house to be kept and cared for until the court could thoroughly review the charges filed against me.

he first morning I woke up in Mrs. Fitzgerald's house, I was taken by the quietness.

The shootout in the high meadow of the Sapphires with the constant *whop whop whop* of the helicopters, the sirens wailing like banshees from hell, Johnny-boy's excited barking, the screams of the injured sheep (yes, it did seem to me they were screaming), the shooting of the rifle as I put down the sheep on fire—well, all that was behind me now. The beautiful quiet surrounding me was as welcomed as the warm comforter which lay over me. I purposely kept my eyes closed and floated in the silence.

When I did finally open my eyes I found that I was in a high four-poster bed, and to my delight a black cat jumped up at the foot. He made no sound. Only the depression on the covers and the extra weight on my feet gave the cat's presence away. On padded paws the cat slowly wound its way to my uncovered head, where I could now hear the deep, vibrating purr in the cat's throat.

I stuck a hand out of the covers. The cat pushed a greeting against it, and my other hand swept down the cat's greasy-looking coat. Sleek and beautiful, the ebony cat sank beneath my touch and purred even louder.

"Who are you?" I asked, almost expecting the cat to answer.

"That's Mr. Tidbit," came the answer from the half-open bedroom door.

There stood Mrs. Emily Wayne Fitzgerald, the nice lady I'd

had met yesterday afternoon.

She wore a blue flower print dress, short in the sleeves that gathered around her abundant upper arms. She wasn't fat, but then again she wasn't thin, either. The white hair springing in short curls about her head made her look a little like a giant Q-tip. Over her dress hung a soiled apron of burnt orange. I thought how much those colors reminded me of a football team.

"I'm making blueberry pancakes and have a ration of crisp bacon to go with them," said Mrs. Fitzgerald.

Mr. Fitzgerald had been in the logging business in the Bitterroot and had, with some hard luck, been rolled over by a freshly cut Ponderosa Pine.

"It was his favorite pine," Mrs. Fitzgerald had explained the night before, as if that had made a difference. It crushed every bone in his body.

"Now, you get up. There's a robe for you in the top of the dresser. Come into breakfast when you finish in the bathroom."

It seemed ludicrous to me that they entrusted the John Dillinger of ten-year-olds to this mild-mannered lady in her early 70s, but things had stopped making sense to me since the day my parents had been killed.

After relieving myself in the hallway bathroom, I padded my bare feet down the smooth hardwood floor in the direction of Mrs. Fitzgerald's kitchen noises.

Mr. Tidbit followed in my footfalls, stopping and smelling the waxed floor, then racing on to the next smell of interest.

The kitchen was bright and cheerful. A cat clock with the cat's tail as the pendulum swept the spot on the wall above the stove. It was 8:15. I had been able to the astonishment of my mom and dad, to tell time by the age of four.

Time was running out, I thought to myself as I sat in front of the place mat on the other side of the table, away from the half-filled coffee cup.

Mrs. Fitzgerald picked up the coffee cup and knocked it back like it was a shot of tequila. Who knows, maybe it was! Her husband's death benefits barely put him in the ground at the cemetery on West Main Street, just across the bridge that spans the icy Bitterroot River. His Social Security was not much, and she still had the payments on the gravestone erected over William's grave.

The only way she could make ends meet was to offer her home as a respite house for unruly children. She had managed fine with most of the children, the majority thinking after their incarceration they had died and gone to TV home heaven.

As she told me all of this, it finally hit me who Mrs. Fitzgerald reminded me of—Aunt Bee from *The Andy Griffith Show*.

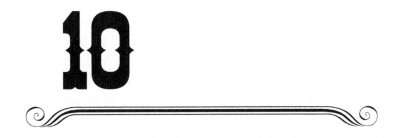

There was a hearing. It was like a trial, but not like any trial I'd ever seen on TV. The court- appointed lawyer seemed to simply agree with everything that Judge Rutherford B. Langston said.

The prosecution recounted the events since my parent's death. But they got it all wrong. Yes, I had laughed when I saw my parents in their coffins, but the way the prosecution told the tale, he made it seem it was the hard laugh of a son making fun of his dead parents. How could the court or the prosecutor or even the judge understand?

How could anyone understand that my parents were also laughing *with me*? And when the church's elder had pulled me from my family fun, how could they not see my parent's disappointment in the callous treatment of the only remnant of flesh that those particular two people had left on earth?

Then there was the retelling of my horse thieving. The most awesome experience, the one experience which I needed above all else, my meeting with the cowboy. Why hadn't the rancher seen the cowboy on his painted horse and his cross-drawn pistol as he jumped the fence first, and me and my paint had merely followed?

Hadn't I followed the cowboy to Calf Creek? Followed him as we evaded the sheriff deputies and followed his direction all the way to Conrad and Johnny-boy?

Why did Conrad take the horse back to the rancher? Why did Conrad betray the boy who had helped him all summer long?

Conrad was on the witness stand now. His eyes were sad and he only glanced in my direction. When I tried to look him in the eyes, Conrad moved his gaze. I instinctively knew they, the authorities, had something on him. The prosecutor kept asking Conrad if he ever touched me. Conrad denied touching me. He denied it vehemently! Surely, the prosecutor and the judge were talking about a different kind of touching. For surely Conrad remembered shaking me early in the morning, and what about when me and Conrad had played tag with Johnny-boy? How could I have ever been "it" if I hadn't been touched?

I guessed the court was talking about some illegal form of touching, but for the life of me I couldn't imagine a touch that would be against the law.

My attorney was asking me to stand up. Judge Rutherford B. Langston was speaking, but I hadn't heard what he'd said. I was still thinking about that illegal touching.

Finally, through the fog of it all, I heard the judge's harsh words.

"Are you listening to me, boy? Or is there more wrong with you than we had imagined?"

I looked up. I looked into the judge's eyes and from there into the judge's very soul. What I saw was not pretty, but certainly it wasn't as ugly as the judge imagined. What I saw was a dirty, scared, little boy who wanted his mother's love. He wanted the love of a mother who could not love. And that shameful secret the judge lived every minute of every day.

The judge stopped speaking as I, a ten year old boy, invaded his soul. For just a moment the judge's mind and my mind became the same thing. I saw a boy who had lived next door to the judge when he was little. How the judge and that boy had clung to each other and loved each other as only survivors of great disasters can do. Then the boy and his family moved away. I don't know how I knew this, I just did.

"Son," the judge began, his voice breaking. "You will be taken from this place, taken from the respite house, and driven by sheriff's deputies to the Rock Ranch Boys Home outside Great Falls, Montana. You will be remanded to that place, working, eating, and living there for the next eight years, until you reach the age of eighteen."

The gavel sounded like a rifle shot, the bullet of which penetrated my heart, destroying any chance of having a normal life again.

Sheriff Deputy's car pulled up in front of Mrs. Fitzgerald's house. The deputy escorted me to the front porch, where Mrs. Fitzgerald and Mr. Tidbit sat. The old lady was rocking and working on her needlepoint. The cat had his forepaws tucked under him, daring anyone to take his place.

"I'll be waiting in the car," the deputy said.

Mrs. Fitzgerald got up and opened the front door for me. Mr. Tidbit eyed the open door but remained where he was.

Inside the room I'd stayed was an open suitcase on the bed. The old woman and I carefully packed the small amount of clothes she'd gathered for me in the open case.

"Have you ever had any other boys sent to Rock Ranch?"

"A few."

"You ever hear from them again?"

"Most boys are not in the habit of contacting places they only stayed a couple of nights."

"Why didn't you and Mr. Fitzgerald foster somebody for a longer period of time?"

"Mr. Fitzgerald didn't want children."

"Oh."

"I like you John."

"I hardly know you Mrs. Fitzgerald, but you seem like a nice lady."

I think she wanted to give me some advice; maybe she'd awakened last night and had actually come up with things she could tell me. Lying in bed last night when she couldn't sleep she probably told herself to get up and write those things down, but the bed had been so comfy and warm and the advice so sagacious, how could she not remember, yet, here she was, not remembering.

"Well," she said, then sort of trailed off.

"Do you know anything about Rock Ranch?"

"I know many boys don't learn their lesson there."

"What's that mean?"

"It means they get in trouble again after leaving Rock Ranch."

"What kind of trouble?"

"All kinds," she said looking a lot like she could end the conversation. "You see, there are no guards there, or prison walls, it's a ranch out in the middle of nowhere."

"Why don't kids just walk off the ranch?"

"They do. That's the problem. The wilderness which surrounds them it's full of all sorts of beasts."

"What do you mean, beasts?"

"Pumas and grizzlies."

"Oh. No one ever escaped?"

"Usually within a couple of days the boys who run away come back with stories of being chased by bears. Well, they never did find two boys who escaped together. Even though there were stories about these boys making it all the way to Canada, most everyone knew they probably ended up as bear scat on the side of some slope."

The ride to the Rock Ranch Boys Home was mostly a blur.

Shortly after Mrs. Fitzgerald kissed me on the head and the deputy had helped me into the back seat and buckled me in I'd gone to sleep. I didn't much care for the mesh screen that separated me from the deputy. It looked like one of us was in a cage, the problem was, which one?

I wondered if the cowboy was following me to Rock Ranch. Surely the cowboy's horse could run fast, but faster than the deputy's car? Probably not. At one point I strained my eyes to see if the cowboy were atop his horse, galloping along the grasses beside the road.

Finally, I fell asleep and somewhere in my sleep I unbuckled my seatbelt and made myself comfortable stretched out on the back seat.

While I slept I had this dream: I dreamed I was riding on the paint I'd first met the cowboy on.

It was early morning, and the sun had not yet met the swales and was only shining on the upper reaches of the mountains. The air was cool, and the trail narrowed as it ascended. Up ahead there was another rider, but each time I thought I'd catch a glimpse of him the trail would turn or ascend again and all I would see was the back of the horse as it disappeared up the trail. The last bit of trail vanished as two mountains came together, forcing the rider to kick his horse up the side of the mountain.

My paint was anxious to follow and with just a bit of encouragement, climbed behind the first rider.

I leaned forward in my saddle and grabbed a handful of dark mane, the horse hair flaring through my closed fingers.

It was a most amazing feeling. The horse, my paint, was striding up the slope with gargantuan steps and actually went faster as the slope became steeper.

When the first rider rounded of the top of the mountain, I could no longer hear or see a glimpse of him. My paint spilled out on the grassy meadow, with the morning sun in full display. The sound of the paint's lungs gasping for breath filled the air, and I saw who I was following.

It was the cowboy! But this time the cowboy was a black man with a long curly beard. He was dressed like a cowboy. I knew it was this same cowboy I'd seen before even though he didn't look the same. The wave of feeling coming off the cowboy was identical, and so was the way he was dressed, right down to the cross drawn pistol. I felt surrounded and submerged in love.

The black cowboy stopped his white horse. I hadn't remembered the horse being white. He waited for me to catch up. His horse danced in a circle as I approached on the paint.

"We're going to catch those who have gone against our way," the black cowboy said, his voice still full of love.

"What will we do to them?" I asked in the dream.

The black cowboy smiled then replied, "We will destroy them."

Try as I may, I cannot remember my first week at Rock Ranch.

What saved me were the trees and the sky. When things were going bad, and boy were they going bad, I looked to the trees and sky. Those trees had been there before Rock Ranch was even conceived of. That sky, painfully blue, penetrating into my eyes, and its friends, the clouds, had been chasing each other across Montana since the time the herds of buffalo were as numerous as the stars.

When adults were yelling instructions and the other boys were laughing and punishment was surely on the way, I developed the thousand-yard-stare of those cauterized in battle. What was being said to me, no shouted into my very face, meant nothing when looked at from the viewpoint of the congregation of trees and the choir of clouds and the firmament of blue sky.

Words had surely been screamed under these skies before. People had been injured, even killed, as the sangha of trees witnessed. But those screams of anger and agony were like dust in the wind—sounds blown away by racing clouds as the gentle whisperings of the wind high in the Pines replaced them.

I had stopped eating. They couldn't force me to eat. I lost weight and rude nicknames were emerging—skeleton boy, spider legs, and the list went on and on. No one, especially not the adults, seemed to care the new boy was being abused. Rock Ranch was run as many boys ranches were—on a pecking order. The more I stood my ground, the more and harder they pecked. I would, I figured, in the end be reduced to nothing.

My dream of the cowboy riding his magnificent steed, voicing to me that my enemies would be destroyed, seemed now to be a cruel joke. Was I only to feel his presence in my dreams? I suspect the trees, the blue sky, and the racing clouds gave me some reflection of the cowboy's peace, but I longed for a vision of the cowboy, if only again in a dream.

But every night brought no dreams. Every night brought living nightmares, further abuse from the other and older boys. I slept only in snatches and was more times than not snatched from my slumbers to endure more and brutal abuse than what the daytime offered.

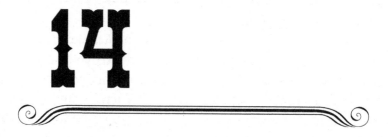

I was sleepwalking through the days. I could've cared less if I lived or died, and between the weight loss and my general apathy, I sincerely hoped I would soon be gone. Besides, perhaps it was time for the little boy who'd lost his parents to join them in death.

I don't even remember why they were abusing me that particular day. Two boys were hitting me on the side of the head with their open palms, making my ears ring and probably causing some sort of permanent hearing loss, but right in the middle it stepped a young negro boy of probably thirteen years. In one swift movement, both of my tormentors were knocked to the ground.

"Anybody else feel like bothering this white boy?" the young negro man asked rather politely.

The crowd dispersed. There were no takers. Just behind the crowd of cheering boys stood several of the foremen of the ranch. They had probably been standing there all along, watching my torture. As far as I knew they could have been standing there every time I'd been messed with by the other boys, but this time they stepped forward and grabbed both my arm and the arm of the young black angel. Yes, I couldn't help but think of the young negro boy as my very own guardian angel.

We were spirited off to the headmaster's office. Above the headmaster's door was a sign that read: "Boss Man."

We were placed in front of the boss man's desk, which was half the size of Montana, and the boots which projected from the boss man's side of the desk were as long as a child's snow skis.

"Leave us!" the boss man barked, and the foreman left immediately.

"You got yourself a slave, Mr. Barnes?"

I looked up, unsure as to what the boss man was talking about.

"Is this your nigger, Mr. Barnes?"

The boy standing beside me flinched when the boss man used the "n" word.

"Mr. Barnes may not be able to hear you, sir. They were bashing his ears pretty bad," said my guardian angel.

"So you're not only got yourself a nigger, you got yourself a house nigger. That's excellent, Mr. Barnes, excellent!"

My glare was tight. The boss man's bushy mustache hid his lips but behind them you could see his tobacco stained teeth.

"Well, Mr. Barnes, let's hope your house nigger has got some field nigger experience cause the two of you are now responsible for the care and feeding of the forty horses here at Rock Ranch. You will eat, sleep, and live with the horses. You're lucky I don't make you eat hay."

The boss man pushed a button on his desk and we could all hear it in the outer office. The foreman who brought us came in and stood behind where we stood.

"These boys will now be eating, sleeping, and living in the barn with the horses. They are to feed and care for the horses, and the stalls are to be mucked every day." The boss man took a cigar from the box on his desk. He bit off the end and spit it expertly into the trashcan alongside his desk.

As we were walked from the office, the boss man said, "One other thing."

The foreman turned us by our shoulders so we faced the boss man. "The next time I see you two boys in here will be the day the nigger turns eighteen. Until then your friends will be the horses. Your teachers will be the horses. Your parents, your brothers and sisters, aunts and uncles, granddads and grandmas will be the horses. Do you both understand?"

I was fairly sure I'd misunderstood everything. Could the boss man have said what he said? Had the boss man essentially put me exactly where I wanted to be? Could I have become Br'er Rabbit? Were the barn and stalls now to be the briar patch? Was the young man beside me not only my guardian angel but also the tar baby?

We were taken to the barn and stall area. When we arrived, our stuff—our clothes and sundries—was already there. Bunk beds in the tack room smelled of linseed oil and leather. I immediately liked the place. Not so much the young negro boy.

"Where do we shower and where's the bathroom?" he wanted to know.

"There is a hose for watering the horses. You can heat water on the stove there," the foreman pointed to an ancient potbellied stove in the corner of the tack room. "I believe there is an empty water trough you can use as a bathtub."

"Where's that? It sure ain't in here..."

"It's out in the stall area."

"We'll freeze in the wintertime!"

"Then be quick about your bathing and get back in here. Plenty of wood for the stove in the stall area. There's two of you and two of them stoves—one at each end of the paddock area. When the weather gets brutal you'll want to keep those babies going around-the-clock. Don't let them go out or it's your hide."

"Do we eat with the other boys?" the boy asked.

"No. Go to the back of the kitchen and you'll get plates. Bring them in here and eat."

"Don't you believe in civil rights?"

"Ain't no civil rights at Rock Ranch! Do as you're told or suffer, and I do mean suffer, the consequences."

The foreman turned and walked out the door leaving it open behind him.

"I get the upper bunk. Don't want no kid peeing on me in the middle of the night," the negro boy declared.

"I haven't wet my bed since I was four."

"That long ago?" the boy said as he jumped on the upper bunk and stretched his long angular frame out.

"My name's John. John Barnes."

"Dwight Farber," he said in reply.

"You didn't have to help me."

Dwight sat up and dangled his legs off the top bunk. "You fond of hearing? If I hadn't stepped in you might not hear anything but a ringing noise the rest of your life."

"Well, I sure do thank you."

"Lot of good it did me," Dwight said as he lay back once again on his bunk.

"Believe it or not this is better than the dorms."

"Yeah, right!"

"Well, you might think so if you were unlucky enough to be picked on in the dorms."

"Boy!" Dwight nearly yelled, sitting up once again. "Nobody picks on me. My folks and I lived on the street and we'd still be there if only..."

"If only?"

"Never you mind. It's personal."

"OK. Personal is fine by me."

"What's that smell?"

"Which one? There are so many wonderful smells out here."

"You're shittin' me, right?"

"Not really. There is the smell of horseshit. Sure smells a lot better than our stuff—"

"Speak for yourself!"

"There's the smell of their pee in the hay and then there's the smell of the horses themselves—"

"They stink!"

"I love that smell, it reminds me of petunias."

"That's flowers!"

"Yeah, when you smell a petunia real deep, take it all into your lungs—right at the bottom of that smell is the same smell as a horse."

"Great! I got a flower–smelling horse lover as a roommate!"

"Do you know how to ride?"

"I ain't getting' on one of those beasts!"

"You'd like it!"

"I would not. I'll never get on no horse!"

15

We were up early. I was showing Dwight how the bales of hay break off into sections.

"They call these sections 'flakes.' Each horse gets four flakes in the morning and four in the evening. We have to make sure some dominant horse doesn't bully another horse and eat his hay."

"They're in different rooms, man, how's that going to happen?"

"There called stalls, not rooms."

"So do we live in a stall?"

"No, that's the tack room, silly."

"What's tack?"

"The stuff that goes on a horse; the saddle, blanket, the head stall, the bit, the reins—actually those three are usually together."

"Oh yeah, the leather strips you steer the horse with?"

"Those are called reins and they're attached to the bit and the bit is attached to the headstall."

"Am I gonna have to take notes?"

I looked at Dwight and smiled.

"You seem like a pretty smart guy. You'll learn this in no time."

We woke at dawn. Dwight started at one end of the stalls and me at the other. The routine was well learned and easy for both of us. I seemed more comfortable with the horses; talking to them in muted tones and stroking each one. But even Dwight became comfortable around the big animals occasionally reaching up and touching one of them.

I put several horses in a very large wooden round pen. I stood in the middle and cracked a buggy whip to get them all going in the same direction. I used the whip—not to hit them, but to get them stopped and going in the opposite direction.

I invited Dwight into the round pen. Dwight joined me and took several turns using the buggy whip to get used to it. Soon Dwight had the horses exercising to his commands. I patted my friend on the back. Dwight smiled at his own accomplishment.

Dwight learned quickly how to properly muck a stall. At first, Dwight stood there holding his nose and not working. I took my bandanna out of my back pocket and tied it around Dwight's face. Then we both began filling the wheelbarrow.

One morning I put one of the horses in the big wooden round pen. I coaxed Dwight to come into the pen. He entered but seemed at the least suspicious and at the most scared. He'd worked the horses in the round pen, but this horse had a saddle on it. I explained to Dwight what to do to actually get on the horse. Dwight put his left foot into the stirrup, but when he started to mount, the horse began walking away.

I pulled on the reins and brought the horse's attention back to the moment.

I encouraged Dwight to put his foot back in the stirrup and swing up. Good. Dwight was mounted. I took the reins and led the horse around the round pen. I gave Dwight some orders and he held his arms out parallel to the ground. I congratulated Dwight on his balance.

Finally, I had Dwight pick up the reins as I moved to the center of the round pen.

"Give her a little punch in her side," I said.

Dwight bent over in the saddle and punched the horse in the side with his fist.

"No, with your heels, dummy!"

Dwight put his heels into the horse. It began to move around the round pen.

"Click 'em up!" I called.

"Man, you might as well be speaking a foreign language."

"Click, click," I demonstrated with my mouth what to do.

Dwight clicked up his horse.

"Now, try both of them together."

Dwight clicked up the horse and put his heels into the horse's side. The horse took off in a trot.

"Now we're talking some speed," Dwight said with an evident amount of glee.

"You want speed?" I asked.

"Oh yeah, the faster the better," Dwight answered

I popped the buggy whip.

The horse took off in a lope.

"Yikes!" Dwight said as he dropped the reins and grabbed hold of the horn.

"How am I doing" Dwight asked.

"You've got one leg on each side and you ain't fell off!"

"That's good, huh?" Dwight said, holding onto the horn for dear life. It was winter. The snow was a couple of feet deep surrounding the round pen area and pasture.

After his ride, we stood by the pasture watching the horses run in the snow. Snow flew as the horses galloped. Their long tails looked like clotheslines trailing after them.

We looked at each other and smiled. We were hooked.

We two boys, Dwight and I, whether we knew it or not were growing up like brothers. Our banishment to the stables had been our ultimate salvation. I no longer thought about Br'er Rabbit and Br'er Fox and the fact that I had once categorized Dwight as my very own tar baby. All those thoughts were gone. Now, when Dwight looked into the mirror he was surprised to see he was black and when I looked in that same mirror I was surprised to see that I was white. A strange and wonderful thing had happened; both of us, in the process of becoming ourselves, had become each other.

Three years had passed. Three beautiful years in which we had become young men and both of us had become nearly expert riders. The absolute thrill of it all was that our only teachers were the remuda of horses kept at Rock Ranch.

It was a blessed time, not only for us, but, quite frankly, for the horses. Before we were banished to the barn's tack room and our only friends became each other and the horses, the horses had been more ornamentation than anything else at Rock Ranch. And believe it when I tell you, the horses knew that. What the horses knew now was the genuine love and admiration of two young men and because of it, the horses flourished.

Unheard of at Rock Ranch, the mares foaled and we were there to help pull skinny, shiny new colts' and fillies' legs from their mothers' bodies. Care and heartfelt attention was paid upon the horses and they responded in kind.

There is an old saying: When the student is ready, the

teacher appears. In this case the teachers were the horses and in gentle and sometimes not so gentle ways, the horses took us metaphorically under their wings and showed us the secrets of the equine world.

Whether you know this or not horses have always considered themselves smarter than humans. To their delight, we two boys knew this fact from the get-go. I think the horses were surprised at our humility and gratified by our humbleness. They literally opened their hearts to us and invited us in.

I was so surprised the first day I saw the cowboy again on his steed. I didn't have the time to tell Dwight about the cowboy, we simply rode the fence line together. The cowboy on one side and both of us on the other. I had so many questions to ask the cowboy, like where he'd been and what he'd been up to, but I was so gratified he'd found me that I simply kept my mouth shut.

There was a lot of smiling going on over that fence and as the ranch people say, "That cowboy was 100% wool and a yard wide!"

I spilled my guts to Dwight that night. I told him all about the first time I'd seen the cowboy. Actually, I told my entire story and in reply Dwight's heart was open to tell his.

Dwight told me of the mean streets of Haight-Ashbury where love was preached but hatred practiced. Of his mixed-race parents—his mother white, his father black—about their escape from small-town society in Wyoming to the supposedly love-drenched streets of the Haight. Dwight told of his life on the streets, his parents doing as best they could under the circumstances, of his father's turning to selling pot and the anger this incurred from local drug lords until those same drug lords turned their guns on the young couple, leaving Dwight not only homeless, but also orphaned.

And so it was. We took on the teacher horses and the teacher horses took us on—it was a match made in heaven.

We turned into young men and then we turned into

horsemen. The lessons learned would foster us the rest of our lives.

What need had we of parents?

And then. Something we'd not counted on nor dreamed of happened.

There was good news and there was bad news. Most people want the good news first. Some want the bad.

Actually, there were two bits of good news, so I will tell both first then will come the bad news.

A wealthy supporter of Rock Ranch died. Yes, this is part of the good news. In her will she gave money and nearly everything else she had to Rock Ranch. She had never had children and dreamed her final wishes would support and enliven the lives of bad boys who were turning good. As a matter of fact, it did.

Among the things she bequeathed to Rock Ranch were a yearling and a mare. Unbeknownst to the dead woman or to Rock Ranch, when they received the two horses the mare was pregnant.

The yearling was a Missouri Foxtrotter and she was a filly. Her mother had been sold before the rich woman's death and she had been—as it were— adopted by the mare as her second mother.   We were thrilled at the prospect of training a yearling and each of us secretly dreamed the yearling would grow up and become our own horse.

Always wanting to please my best friend and protector, I had finally told Dwight the yearling was his to train and ride.

Dwight was awestruck. He never imagined his new, younger friend could be so giving. But there I was giving to Dwight what he knew I wanted. If nothing else it cemented our friendship even more than it was before.

The second good thing to happen—if we're talking the order in which things appeared—was that the Appaloosa mare named

CC's Black Gold was pregnant. Not more than six weeks after the rather rotund mare arrived, we were surprised to see another filly.

The sun was coming up over the Crazy Woman Mountains. The sky was filled with oranges, reds, streaks of deep purple, all against a backdrop of painfully blue sky. In world geography we'd been studying South America, and as the foal came slipping out, I looked into the sunrise. This little filly deserved a name worthy of this magnificent morning. And then it came to me literally out of the blue, "Santiago Sunrise." We would call her "Tia" for short. Yes, some people would imagine she was some Mexican's horse and perhaps some other horse's aunt, but Dwight and I would know what "Tia" meant.

Within moments Tia was standing on wobbly legs. She had a splash of white on her face which angled to the right as you looked at her. White socks adorned three of her feet. I knew as Tia stood there, the sunrise fading a bit behind her, that my life and the life of this little filly would be entwined forever.

I wondered where the cowboy was at this auspicious occasion, then like a lightning flash it came to me. On some level, I had taken the cowboy inside me! The cowboy I admired and worshipped had become my beacon, my load star, my compass, and I, having the will to become the best I could be, had become the cowboy. True, I didn't carry a cross drawn six-shooter, nor did I have his panache, but many times when I held my mouth just so, and had my cowboy hat tipped back on my head, I could have sworn I was him.

Now, I understood. Yes, I was sure I would see the cowboy again, I was sure I would speak to the cowboy again in person, and most of all I was absolutely sure I would be sitting on Santiago Sunrise when I did so.

And then a most amazing thing happened... China, the Missouri Foxtrotter sorrel filly, came over and began to suckle Tia's mother, CC's Black Gold.

Tia's mother was neither surprised nor offended and Tia

simply stood in line, like a good girl. When China had finished her turn, she licked the remnants of the afterbirth off Tia's hind quarters.

We proud fathers watched our children. We two young men and our horses had come from many different directions to end up at this singular place.

As all good stories are wont to do the minute a perfect balance is struck, something happened to throw things off-kilter. And that something came in the form of an older white couple driving at that precise moment beneath the ranch gate of Rock Ranch. We didn't know it at the time, and I think if we would have, we would have taken off from Rock Ranch. But the future is not known by anyone but God the Father. The rest of us are left to trudge our way through regardless of the circumstances. Unfortunately for Dwight and I, this older white couple was the bad news amongst the good.

The elderly couple making their way through the ranch gate at Rock Ranch in their late model Buick Skylark were as surprised as anyone that they were there.

Of course, I found all this out much later, but their young daughter had fallen in love with a young black boy and when neither set of parents got on board with that notion, the salt-n-pepper couple had simply disappeared.

Foul play was hinted. At first, both sets of parents pointed their fingers at the other. The Sheriff of Cheyenne County investigated, but all he could find out was the couple had been seen at the bus station. Oddly, no bus station employee or bus driver could remember a young black and white couple traveling together.

Those young teenage kids had been smart. The fifteen year old white girl had boarded the Oakland, California bus early and sat up front. The driver remembered her not because she was pretty—which she was—but mostly because she'd been so polite. That same driver hadn't remembered the young black man who got on mostly because he was prejudiced against niggers of any age and had made a habit in the past twenty-some years to ignore them unless they caused a problem, then he would give them some shit.

The couple had gotten off the bus separately in Oakland and by that time the driver had changed three times. The final destination driver was, in fact, a black man. Even if Dwight's mom and dad had been seated directly behind him he would have cared less. Live and let live was his motto.

After five years the teenagers' pictures stopped appearing at the Post Office and both the black parents and the white parents had given up hope and come through an uncertain grief realizing that most likely their children were dead.

The husband of the black couple had been killed in a drilling accident and the wife, after collecting his insurance, moved back to Mississippi to take care of her elderly parents and forgot about her sojourn into America's heartland, America's West.

Dwight's maternal grandparents, Rick and Barbara Anderson, had given up and would have left things as they were had not Dwight's grandfather had an army buddy from Korea who fancied himself a detective. Carl Mayor and Rick Anderson were two of the handful who had survived the Battle of Bloody Ridge back in August of 1951. That left some emotional damage, but Carl simply went on and on and in his going onward he took to checking police and military files, looking for human puzzles to solve. Ever since the disappearance of Rick and Barbara Anderson's daughter, Carl had been working on finding the young girl. At first Carl would call Rick and give him whatever news he had, but Rick didn't seem to care much, so Carl stopped telling his Korean War buddy what he'd found until he found out about the grandchild, Dwight.

The Andersons later told Dwight about the day Carl came over to see them. How the Mrs. had gotten Carl a glass of tea and put some of Carl's favorite cookies out—chocolate chip—and how Carl had simply sipped the tea and not touched the cookies. They knew something bad was up when Carl didn't touch the cookies. Even after Mrs. Anderson pushed them a little closer to Carl, he had simply grunted and not picked one up. Really—that said it all.

After Carl had left, Mrs. Anderson moved over and sat where Carl had been sitting and in some sort of replacement ritual, she'd sat there and ate all seven chocolate chip cookies before she and her husband spoke.

There was never a question of *what* they would do—they were, in a sense, the perfect couple and as the perfect couple, they would do the right thing. The details of the right thing were worked out over the next week and a half.

First they called Rock Ranch. The people in charge had to be notified and they were. Telling the in-charge people at Rock Ranch that Dwight was their biological grandson led the older couple to assume certain things. For example: They assumed Dwight would be informed that his grandparents were coming to pick him up and take him back to their home, where they also assumed he would lead a better life and be grateful to them the rest of his days. But that's the trouble with assumptions. We conjecture in this way and, none of these conjectures are based on any sort of reality.

Army Drill Sergeants are famous for saying, "When you assume, you make an ass out of you and me."

That's not far from the truth in this instance. Not far at all.

For as their late model Buick drove under the ranch gate at Rock Ranch Dwight was, in fact, the happiest he'd ever been his entire life. I knew that and he knew that. He was about to be pulled directly out of the horse-ranching life he'd come to learn and love. In the next few years he'd never come any closer to it than the penny pony at the supermarket. A foundation had been laid. Taking into account all the disappointment and frustration he was about to experience and the loneliness of being separated from his best friend and from his horse, that foundation would remain the rest of his life. He would forever be grateful for it. Dwight might have started out as the child of hippie-runaways, but at Rock Ranch he'd become, with my help and the horses as teachers, a cowboy.

But none of this wisdom would register at first, not a speck. He was literally about to be pulled from cowboy paradise to a sterile, white people's hell, and gratitude was the last thing old Dwight's heart was ready to express.

When the head of Rock Ranch took the Andersons to the stable I imagine they were taken aback by where Dwight slept. Probably, if it hadn't been for me rooming in the same small space both Mr. and Mrs. Anderson would have surely thought there was some sort of open discrimination going on.

Neither of us boys could figure out what was up.

When the head honcho brought the older white couple back to the stables, we both thought they were generous donors receiving a tour. Hell, we were both so high on our new horses we could have cared less.

We both started talking at them before the couple was even completely into the room. Then I stopped and deferred to Dwight since; 1) Dwight was older, and 2) Dwight was my protector. You never could tell who you needed protection from, maybe; I even needed protection from this older, white couple?

"It may seem as if the two of us have it bad out here in the stables," Dwight began, his future-to-be grandparents giving him all their attention, "but someone has to keep an eye on the horses. Not only do they need to be fed twice a day, but there are other needs they have which must be tended to." Dwight paused, out of gas at this point.

"Such as," I gestured to the well-cared for tack which lined the walls, "the saddles, headgear, reins, bits and saddle blankets all need care. The saddles, head stalls and reins must be wiped down with Neatsfoot oil, then the extra oil wiped off. The saddle blankets are usually wet with the horses sweat and they need to be dried out before storing them one on top of the other—"

"Boys," the headmaster began, "Mr. and Mrs. Anderson are not here to be impressed by the wonderful job you're both doing at the stables and you're certainly doing a great job—"

It was the first time in three years that not only had the headmaster, or anyone else for that matter, said anything positive about the job we were doing, but in truth, it was the first time we'd even seen the headmaster in the barn and stable area.

The headmaster looked around, not sure what to say next. Finally, he spoke directly to me. "John, why don't you go do the horse chores? I think Mr. & Mrs. Anderson need time alone with Dwight."

I stepped outside. The day was cold and it wasn't until I was standing out there I noticed I hadn't brought my jean jacket with me.

I was thinking hard about whether I should go in and get my jacket before I got cold, but before I could move, the door to the tack room opened and the older white couple walked out with Dwight in between them.

Our eyes met. I smiled and Dwight smirked and rolled his eyes. I wasn't sure what that meant, but I knew it couldn't be good.

Dwight looked over his shoulder one last time and raised an open palm in my direction. As if to say, "What are you going to do about this?"

I raised my open palm in response, seconds before the threesome disappeared around the corner of the barn.

The headmaster stood halfway between me and the disappearing threesome.

"Where are they going?" I asked. A fairly simple question really.

"They're taking Dwight away," the headmaster said in a flat tone.

"To lunch?"

"To a whole lifetime of lunches, he's being adopted."

"What?"

"You heard me," was all the headmaster offered.

I broke into a run, but was easily outmaneuvered by the bigger man. The headmaster grabbed me and held on tight.

"Let me go! Do you hear me, let me go!"

The headmaster didn't answer, he simply waited until he saw the white, late-model Buick round the corner and head up toward the ranch gate. Then, he let me go.

I ran as fast as I could across the plush grass which seemed to be tugging at my boots. Once I made the main road I picked up speed, but it was useless. I knew I'd never catch that car. I could see Dwight's face in the back window as Dwight raised his open palm in friendship as the car turned onto the state highway.

Of course, what the older couple had expected, the best case scenario, was my buddy Dwight running into their open arms. What they had expected had not matched up to the event. Dwight, incredulous, had to nearly be dragged to the car. You'd think an orphan would run from the orphanage, run to the possibility of a normal life.

It wasn't until much later I found out the cowboy had seen everything—all of it. It made the cowboy sad that we all would not be riding together any time in the near future. In a sense for the cowboy the future was just a moment away. I know that seems hard to understand as I'm telling you this, Mariah, but the cowboy, it turns out, was smarter than all of us. He knew what the Andersons didn't know, he knew what the headmaster didn't know, he knew that we boys, as grown men, would be reunited with our horses and we'd all of us, including the cowboy, would be back together again.

But in our world, that was many years away.

I was miserable! I'd run down the road after those old white people who kidnapped Dwight. I'd seen the man's ruddy, strained face in the driver's side rear view mirror. The old man had seen me running after them. Why wouldn't he stop to allow me to say my goodbyes?

Next to my parents' dying this was the worst day of my short life. I'd lost my best friend forever! I was sure I'd never see Dwight again. And, in a way, even worse, Dwight would never have the opportunity to train his horse, China.

It was lonely at night. Real lonely! I didn't complain because I was sure as soon as I complained I would be transferred back to the general population and the regular dorms. Without my protector I was sure the boys would bully me again. Then again, I was older and I'd filled out, and Dwight had made me believe in myself. I wouldn't ever let anyone bully me again. Yet, when a group of boys made up their minds to make your life a living hell there was essentially no way to keep them from trying.

So. The first few nights, I cried myself to sleep. I spent a lot of more time with Tia and China. I made up my mind I'd train China to be Dwight's horse, but I wasn't quite sure how one would do that.

On the fourth night of my new loneliness, when the weather front had come early and the wind was howling, there was a rap at the tack room door.

My heart leapt into my mouth and for one moment I thought it might be Dwight! But what would Dwight be knocking on his own door? Why wouldn't Dwight simply walk on in, kick me off the top bunk, and tell me how he'd escaped from the white people. Old Dwight could spin a yarn, and I was looking forward to hearing about his fantastic escape.

After another short rap, the door eased open and I saw the white hand and fingers on the side of the door before I saw the man's face.

It wasn't anybody I knew. For a moment I thought it might be the cowboy, he was dressed like one, but it wasn't the cowboy. It was a grown man. I imagined he might be as old as thirty!

The man was dressed in boot cut wranglers and wore a western shirt with pearl snap buttons. His boots weren't brand-new, but they weren't old either. The tops of the boots were highly polished above the toe design and some people might think it was from wearing spurs, but I knew from experience your boots got that way from the bottom of your Wranglers brushing back and forth on them a thousand times a day.

The man took off his black Cinch hat and held it in both hands.

"Are you John Wilson Barnes?"

I nodded in agreement.

"The headmaster sent me over to talk to you."

"What about?"

"Things in general. You up for that? Would you like to talk now or would it be better suited for you to talk later?"

"Who are you, anyway?"

"I'm the new Foreman. Name's Charles Dawson. My friends call me Charlie."

"Well, Mr. Dawson, I'd appreciate it if we could talk later."

Charles Dawson had begun unbuttoning his jean jacket and with those words began to button it back up again.

"OK, how about I come early tomorrow and help you with the morning feed?"

"All right."

Dawson put his hat back on his head and opened the door. "Tomorrow it is, then."

That night I had a dream.

In the dream I was standing in an open field. Fog hugged the ground and the rising sun reflected throughout the fog. It was an encircling brightness which lit things up and almost blinded you at the same time.

I could sure smell horses. First it was the wonderful smell of their shit. Im my opinion, when someone screams, "Horseshit!" it seems to me as if they might be approving whatever is going on.

Then came the smell of their flesh, heavy with horse sweat. From the first time I'd ever smelled their sweat I found it intriguing. My nose's first reaction was to flinch away—to pull itself out of the aroma—but if one ruled one's nose, one could keep the smell coming in and there at the bottom of that harsh smell was the surprising smell of petunias. I think I've mentioned that once before, but hell, if you haven't tried it, then you ought to.

I could hear the horses. Their chortling voices deep in their throats, the sudden snorts, and then a quiet whinny. I still couldn't see them, and that worried me because they were starting to gallop and the sound of their galloping was coming my way. The last thing I wanted was to be run over by a remuda of horses.

I whirled around. Sure enough, a horse was about to overrun me. And there it was.

It was the cowboy's paint. It wore an empty saddle, and it was lathered up as if it had been rode hard. Spit flew from its mouth as it pirouetted. The saliva hit me across the face and strangely I felt blessed.

The paint calmed down and moved sideways toward me. I got the impression the horse was telling me to mount up. The stirrups were high on this eighteen hands horse, and as I thought about jumping up there, my legs were moving, pumping as I took three quick steps and leapt toward the stallion.

Much to my surprise I flew through the air. My left foot

planted itself firmly in the stirrup.

Throwing my right leg over the horse's backside I was mounted on eleven-hundred pounds of trembling flesh. The stirrups should've been too long, but either they had been shortened for me or my legs had grown instantly to fill the length.

The cowboy's paint took off in a full gallop through the fog. Momentarily, I felt bad about stealing the cowboy's horse, but then knew I wasn't really stealing anything. The paint had come to deliver me from an unseen danger.

It was at this point I awakened. Unlike many dreams, I remembered all of it. The only lingering question was: What was the danger from which I was being delivered?

The next time I saw Charles Dawson the sky was clear and a robin's egg blue. The sun, bright and warming. It was a beautiful winter's day. I knew to wear sunglasses when the snow was reflecting the sun. Rock Ranch didn't buy me sunglasses. I found them in the tack room. The earpiece on the left side was missing, but I took some baling string and jerry-rigged the glasses around my head. It might have looked ghetto, but no matter what I was doing with the horses the glasses stayed on.

I'd been working with Tia and China in the round pen. I hadn't forgotten whose horse China was. I trained China for Dwight, sure that in some way or other, things would work out. I wasn't sure how, but I knew cowboys always took the worst circumstances and turned them into something good.

Strange as it may seem, back then I thought a lot about the children of Israel and their enslavement in Egypt. Rock Ranch was my Egypt. I was a slave to the state and I would remain one until I was eighteen years old. As such, for the next few years I would keep the Rock Ranch horses and pretend it was all about the horses. Oh, I went to classes—I had to attend classes and make good grades if I wanted to keep my job at the stables. Here's the strange thing about that. Even though Dwight was gone, the other boys seemed to think he might be hiding around the next corner. They actually gave me more respect than when Dwight was there. I wasn't sure what that meant, but I came to the realization that since I'd taken on the cowboy inside me they were seeing something more than just me when they looked my way. I think they knew that me and the cowboy were one.

Charles Dawson rode up that beautiful winter morning on a horse I hadn't seen before. It wasn't one of Rock Ranch's horses that's for sure. It was Charles Dawson's own horse.

Dixie, stood seventeen and a half hands high and was one spirited gelding. In fact, a lot of people who knew the horse had said the horse hadn't calmed down a bit since he was gelded. But I wouldn't know about that.

Charles later confided in me that he'd almost not bought Dixie because the horse was gelded. But Charles rode him anyway, since he'd driven all that way to look at him and he was surprised how much spirit the horse still had. If he'd had the horse from the beginning, he never would've gelded him.

Dawson had on full-length Indian chaps. His cowboy boots had spurs strapped across them and they jiggled even when Dixie was simply walking. Charles wore a winter wool jacket which stopped at his waist. He had a golden silk wild rag tied around his neck. The long silk scarf was tucked into a brown, wool vest. His hands were covered with rough brown leather gloves. The gloves were also lined with wool and even though it might have been the dead of winter in Montana, with the long johns I could see protruding from beneath his shirt, I was sure he felt perfectly comfortable.

"Whatcha doin'?" Charles asked, looking into the round pen.

"What's it look like I'm doing?" was the only reply I made as I continued to work the two green horses.

"You got a good saddle horse in the stables?"

"Got a bunch of 'em."

"Saddle one up and let's go!"

I stopped shaking the buggy whip at China and Tia and they slowed down.

"Where we goin'?"

"Just for a ride, thought maybe you'd like to get far enough from Rock Ranch you couldn't see the buildings."

70

"We aren't allowed to ride that far."

"You'd be with me."

I considered this possibility, but then dismissed it.

"Nah, I got a work these two youngsters."

"We could let 'em into the pasture and they'd follow us."

"How do you know they'd do that?"

"Stop working them, put down the whip and walk over here."

I did exactly that.

"Just as I thought," said Charles Dawson.

"What?"

"Turn around."

To my amazement Tia and China were standing right behind me.

"They've already joined up with you. As far as they're concerned you're the leader of the herd."

"Really?"

"Go saddle up. I'll let them out into the pasture, see for yourself."

Ten minutes later I rode out of the barn area and into the open pasture land. Charles set atop Dixie. Tia and China were feeding nearby.

"What do I do now?" I asked.

"Simply get their attention, then take off. They should be right behind you."

I rode over to where the two fillies were eating. I pulled my paint up sharply beside them. They both looked up while continuing to chew the hay I'd thrown them. I put my heels into the paint and she took off toward the hills several miles away.

Tia turned a circle and ran after me. China was right behind Tia.

"What did I tell you?" whooped Charles Dawson as he touched his spurs to Dixie's side.

We rode pretty far out. As a matter fact, we rode until we could no longer see Rock Ranch. This worried me a little. Dwight and I had been told many times over the past few years not to ride out of sight of the ranch.

I pulled my paint up short. Tia and China settled in behind us and began pawing at the snow to get at the grass.

"We can't see the ranch anymore," I said.

Charles Dawson, who had pulled easily up beside me, put his left hand on the cantle of the saddle and gazed around one-hundred and eighty degrees.

"You're right. It's like Rock Ranch doesn't exist."

"I wish."

"You really wish the ranch wasn't around?" Charles asked, his brow knitted. He was serious, and it was a serious question.

"Nobody likes to be locked up, confined."

"What about horses?"

"What do you mean?"

"They're corralled, locked up, as it were."

"That's different!"

"How's it different?"

"It just is."

"How? It's not different if you can't explain how it's different."

"They don't know they're locked up!"

"Don't they? And why do they escape when someone leaves a gate open?"

"I don't know."

Charles walked his horse sideways so that his right leg and my left leg were nearly touching.

"The point I want to make is this; horses are wild when they're born, right? I mean there is no such thing as a broke colt, right?"

I was considering what Charles had said, but I didn't answer.

"Right?" Charles asked again.

"Right. No such thing as a broke colt."

"Do you think what we do to horses, who are born wild, is bad for them?"

"Without doing what we do, we wouldn't be able to enjoy them."

"That's right. Unless a horse is broke, it can't be ridden. Do you see a similarity between you and the horse?"

"Not really."

"Son, I've read your file. When you came here you were one unbroken colt."

I stared at Charles.

"So... if Rock Ranch wasn't here, would you have ever been broke?"

"Nobody broke me."

"No?"

"No!"

"What about the horses?"

"What about them?"

"Don't you think the horses are glad you arrived here at Rock Ranch? Don't you think they're better off since you've arrived?"

"I take care of them."

"And they, in turn, have taken care of you."

"They didn't break me."

"No? Would you get up at four a.m., every morning, even when it's freezing cold outside? Would you do that for any other reason than them?"

"No. I guess not."

"No guessing about it, son. While you were taking care of them guess what they were doing?"

I looked up at Charles. A lot of what he was saying made sense.

"They were... taking care of me."

"Now you got it," Charles said as he spurred his horse in the direction even further from Rock Ranch.

I heeled the paint and as soon as it'd taken off, Tia and China scurried toward the retreating horses and riders.

24

I wasn't quite sure what to think. No one at Rock Ranch—excluding Dwight, of course—had ever treated me with much respect and consideration. I wanted to believe in Mr. Charles Dawson, but it somehow was too good to be true. If Charles had been the cowboy, I could have believed in him, no problem. As I rode to catch up with him I had two thoughts.

First and foremost was how thrilled I was to be treated as something besides a criminal. I even imagined if my father had only had a long lost brother or distant cousin, then perhaps Charles Dawson would have been that person.

The next thought was keeping me from believing the first thought. That was probably a good thing. For the second thought, the thought which pushed the first thought nearly out of my mind was this; what did Charles Dawson want in return? Or more precisely, why was this grown man treating me with such respect? This thought was about to win over as we reached the perimeter of Rock Ranch. On the other side of that fence lay the outside world, a world where I was simply a young boy.

"There it is," Charles Dawson said.

At first I thought Dawson was talking about the perimeter fence so I said nothing.

"What you think of it, pretty nice, huh?"

I'd seen some fences in my day—hell, I'd jumped a rancher's fence on the rancher's very own horse. Yeah, it was a nice fence as fences go, but not unjumpable, that's for sure.

I'd show him. I turned the paint around in a quick pirouette and traveled back as far as I thought the older horse would need to make the jump.

The expression on Dawson's face was interesting. He was puzzled, that's for sure. His puzzlement would turn to astonishment when the paint and I cleared that fence.

"What are you up to?" Dawson asked.

I smiled as I dug my heels two quick times into the paint's side. The horse took off toward the fence. I couldn't wait to have the feeling of flying over the fence.

I had the feeling of flying again, but this time I was alone. The horse's sudden, complete stop launched me over the saddle horn, over the horse's neck; the reins were ripped from my hands and now my arse end was about to be over my head as I somersaulted into the barbed wire fence.

By the time Charles Dawson had dismounted I realized with a few tugs I was hopelessly caught in one of the perimeter fences at Rock Ranch. Bee stings, or what felt like bee stings, were sending messages to my brain from nearly every conceivable part of my body. I tried to move, but only managed to get myself to cry out in pain.

"Don't move! You'll only make it worse," Charles shouted.

I stopped moving and imagined myself like one of those coyotes who get killed and hung on a rancher's fence to warn off other coyotes. My body would serve as a warning for other kids. They would not be so foolish. They would not try to jump a Rock Ranch fence.

Charles was gently lifting my left arm pulling the stingers from my forearm and shoulder.

"If the horse would have actually decided to make the trip, I think you might have made it."

I tried to laugh, but all laughing did was move my body and moving my body did nothing but cause more pain.

"Don't try to do anything. I won't make any more jokes. Just lie still and while you're lying there answer this question: Why did you try to jump the fence when there's a gate right there?"

"Gate's no challenge."

Charles chuckled to himself.

"I mean, I knew you'd want to see my place, but I didn't realize you'd be in such a hurry."

"Your place?"

Charles pointed across the dirt road.

From where I was impaled upon the fence I could easily see the wood frame ranch house with a small barn, a couple of outbuildings and some pasture.

"That your place?"

"Yeah, what the heck did you think we came out here for?"

China and Tia were standing nervously by watching Charles's ministrations.

I had to laugh to myself. I wasn't sure of anything at this point, least of all why we'd come out here to Charles Dawson's ranch.

The bathroom was larger than any bathroom I'd ever seen in a house. I was sitting on the closed toilet lid in nothing but my underwear. That was weird. At my feet knelt Mr. Charles Dawson.

In one hand he held the bottle of methylate, and in the other he held the bottle of hydrogen peroxide.

My young body was splotched with many barbed wire cuts. Some of them were barely noticeable, and some were angry red cuts which wept my very own life's blood.

"You know what these are?"

"That one," I said pointing to the peroxide, "bubbles in and around and cleans the wound out."

"What about this one?"

"I've never seen that one before."

"Well... this one hurts as much as the peroxide tickles. Can you take a little hurt for the team?"

"Whose team?"

"Our team, son, it's you and me, you and me, we're the team I'm talking about."

"We're a team?"

"I need to be on your side and you need to be on mine, because if we're not a team we can both get into trouble."

"What for? You're helping me out. You rescued me out of that wire."

"But we're not supposed to be off property."

"You just live on the other side of the road."

"Doesn't matter. Off property is off property. So if you want me to help you, there are certain things we have to agree on."

"What things?"

"You've never been to this house. As a matter of fact, you have no idea where I live."

"I'm good with that"

"You fell into the barbed wire fence when we were rounding up stray horses and I've fixed you up at the stables."

"OK. But why all the secrecy?"

"You like me, don't you?"

"Yeah, so?"

"And you know I can teach you more about cowboying than you'd ever hope to learn at Rock Ranch."

"I promise I won't say anything."

"OK. Let's get started."

Charles applied the hydrogen peroxide by pouring it on to the wounds and cleaning them up with gauze. At one point I had to take off my undershirt. I felt almost naked in front of this grown man, but the man was my friend, right? The man was risking his job to help me out. What harm could this man possibly do to me?

Then, I found out. The methylate which Charles swabbed onto each wound burned like an everlasting fire. As the swabbing continued I simply broke down and started crying.

Mr. Dawson took me in his arms. Dawson was kneeling in front of the toilet. I had my head over Charles's left shoulder and the tears were streaming down my cheeks.

I could feel Charles's heartbeat on the other side of his shirt and this both thrilled and scared me.

26

The crying was over. Charles had left me in the bathroom to get dressed and gone into the kitchen to fix us some lunch.

I pulled my jeans on over the many bandages on my legs. I counted the barbed wire cuts. There were seven on one leg and five on the other. Twelve cuts in all. I tried to count the ones on my back by looking into the mirror, but I was too short to see my entire back in it. There were three on my left arm and two on my right and yes, several cuts on my butt. Mr. Dawson had been especially gentle when he put the hurtful, angry liquid on my butt and had blown hard and long to cool the cuts down. I appreciated it at the time, but it also seemed weird.

The closeness we'd shared over the cuts and getting bandaged up was weird, too. Me and Dawson had grown closer and the emptiness I felt over Dwight being taken away was made somewhat less.

Completely dressed now, I'd kept my cowboy hat on the whole time. I headed down the hall toward the kitchen. I could hear Charles in there. There were some pot and pan sounds and the sound of something frying. It smelled good, but I couldn't place what it was.

Halfway down the hall I caught sight of a door opened just an inch. I pushed the door wider and I could see model airplanes hanging from the ceiling. They looked like old-timey planes—the ones with two sets of wings. They weren't just hanging, though. They were staged in an epic battle.

There had to be about one hundred of them hanging at different altitudes and attitudes. Planes with the German swastikas on them were being pursued by American planes. Some planes had bullet holes in the sides of the fuselage where they'd been strafed. One double winged plane's pilot had a scarf around his neck and the scarf was flying out behind the plane as if the wind where pushing by. The rest of the room definitely had the feel of a young boy's room. Beside a double bed there was a blonde upright piano. Music set on the music stand as if the boy who lived there had just finished playing the Sonata, then run out to play baseball with his friends.

The wall opposite the piano was covered with plaques and awards. I walked over for a better look. Over twenty plaques and awards in all. Each bore the same name: Charles Alton Dawson. Most of them were speech awards from the American Legion and a few were citations for excellence in drama. In the corner, a knickknack shelf held large trophies; all of them American legion trophies for speech contests.

On the bed between two pillows—propped up by them really—was a football on which a lot of people had signed their names. I picked it up and started to read the names.

"That's the game ball from my last high school game."

I nearly dropped the ball, and then put it back where it had been, cradled between the two pillows.

"I'm sorry."

"What are you sorry for?"

"The door was cracked and I saw the planes."

"Pretty impressive, huh?"

"Did you make all those?"

"I certainly put them together."

"And the way you hung them up—"

"I know. Cool, huh?"

"Is this your room from when you were a kid?"

"Sort of," Charles said as he put his hand in the middle of my back and nudged me out the door.

"Did you grow up here?"

"Not exactly," Charles said as he closed the door to the room. We were now standing in the hallway.

"I fixed some hamburgers and fries. You hungry?"

At the mention of hamburgers I forgot about the room and its mausoleum atmosphere. I forgot about the diorama which Charles had built to his childhood. Why would a grown man have done something like that to a room? What did it mean?

I forgot about all those things as we sat in the Santa Fe style kitchen with the Kiva burning in the corner. We sat there in the warmth of that kitchen and ate burgers and fries and drank Coca-Cola. I didn't want to think about anything, but my great, good fortune in having a new friend like Charles Alton Dawson.

"I want to write Dwight. Can you find out his address for me?"

"Sure, kid, as soon as we get back to Rock Ranch."

C harles and I had been working with the yearlings, Tia and China, in the arena. They couldn't be ridden yet, but long (really long) reins could be hooked up to hackamores and in this way they could be neck-reined around the arena.

Charles had set up some plastic traffic cones down the middle of the arena and he and I were having a contest. The contest was who could run/walk their horse through the cones, slalom style, without touching one of the cones.

Tia and I had just made a successful run through the cones and now it was Charles and China's turn.

"I miss my friend Dwight. I can't believe he hasn't written me."

"He's probably forgotten all about you," Charles stated flatly as he clicked his tongue and shook the long reins starting China through the cones.

I knew I shouldn't speak while Charles and China did their run, but I couldn't help myself.

"He is my best friend, ever, in the entire, whole world, he wouldn't forget about me."

Charles stopped China halfway through the cone course and turned.

"If Dwight is, in fact, your best friend ever in the entire world, then why hasn't he written you?"

I looked down at the ground and drew a circle with my boot toe around a fresh pile of horse manure.

"Maybe he was *your* best friend, but you weren't his?"

Charles suggested before he clicked China up and through the rest of the course.

I had considered that possibility, but not for very long. If Dwight had lied when he said he was my best friend ever well, then, I didn't even want to think about what that could possibly mean. What was considered the norm around Rock Ranch, both among the foremen and the boys, was this; once someone left the Rock they didn't give the Rock or anyone still there a second thought. I had thought about that option, too, and it was a thought which ate at me each night as I tried to fall asleep.

Things at Rock Ranch went pretty much as usual. I attended my classes and kept the stable and barn area immaculate.

Me and Charles Dawson did a lot together. Charles made sure I was able to stay out of the dorms, at least that's what he told me. That was good, if, in fact, it were true.

I was afraid when Dwight left I would be at the mercy of the older boys, but then again, I was one of the older boys now. Besides, Charles had told me not to worry. Now that Dwight was gone he, Charles, would protect me if I needed the protection.

I was mucking the stalls when Charles showed up. He leaned across the adjacent stall and watched me work for a while before he held up the white envelope.

"Guess what I have?"

I looked up, then I dropped the shovel and dove for the envelope. Charles pulled the letter away and held it above his head.

"Hey!"

"Hey what?"

"You know how long I've been waiting for that letter."

"So?"

"So, I want to read it."

"Let's ride out to my place. We can have lunch and you can read it there."

"That means I have to wait!"

"Yeah, all good things come to those who wait."

I picked up the shovel and threw it in the wheelbarrow.

"What are you doing?" Charles asked.

"I'm going to saddle up my horse—"

"No, no, I'll saddle the horse, you finish mucking."

The ride out to Charles Dawson's ranch took more time than I liked. I tried to kick the roan I was riding now into a lope a couple of times but each time Charles had me back off to a trot and then eventually a walk. The horses certainly weren't going to get tired riding at this pace.

Tia and China instinctively followed me and the roan. I could see the change in the young fillies. As far as I was concerned, China was still Dwight's horse and eventually I would get the Missouri Fox Trotter to Dwight. There are certain dreams young men don't want to let go of, and this was certainly one of them.

When the gate was opened so we could cross the road, Tia and China were right behind me.

Charles closed the gate so Tia and China couldn't leave Rock Ranch property.

"Can't we let them into your paddock area?"

"They're not my horses."

"Yeah, but neither is the one I'm riding."

"They're not haltered up and they're not broke yet."

"They'll follow me just like they always do."

"No."

I reined the roan around pointing back toward Rock Ranch and rode up to the now closed gate.

"Then, I'm not going into your house."

"Then, you won't get to read Dwight's letter."

"I want my horses with me!"

"They're not your horses!"

"They're not yours either!"

It was a standoff.

"Then, open the gate and ride back to Rock Ranch."

"Fine."

I opened the gate and was about to join Tia and China.

"I'll open the gate to the paddock area," Charles said.

Charles crossed the road to the paddock area fence. He managed to lean over and opened the gate without dismounting.

The two fillies, Tia and China, frolicked through the opening and fell in behind the roan as I rode briskly into the paddock area.

Charles closed the paddock gate.

"Just tie up the roan right where you are. I'll see you inside," Charles said as he rode toward his house and the hitching post out front.

The house was warm and cozy. When I came through the front door the fireplace had been built back up from the morning and the logs were crackling nicely.

Charles was heating milk on the stove.

"You like hot chocolate?" he asked as he reached into the cupboard and pulled out the Hershey's chocolate mix.

"Do you know a kid who doesn't?" I said as I hung my jacket on the hall tree and placed my cowboy hat on top of the rack.

Charles was busy at the stove.

"That letter you got from 'your best friend in the whole world' is on the breakfast bar."

I jumped up and grabbed the envelope.

"Hey! It's been opened!"

"John, you know all correspondence from outside Rock Ranch has got to be read by one of the staff."

"Did you read the letter?"

"I did! And it's a good one!"

I opened it and began reading.

Charles set down the hot chocolate in front of me.

"You like marshmallows?"

I nodded without taking my eyes off the letter. Charles generously sprinkled the round tiny clouds on top of my hot chocolate.

The first thing I noticed was it wasn't in Dwight's hand. I'd seen Dwight's homework and knew his sprawling hand which was a cross between printing and writing. I got past the different handwriting by imagining Dwight's grandmother seated at the dining room table scribbling the letter as Dwight spoke the letter out loud.

Dwight was well, the letter said. He lived with his grandma and grandpa in a two-story wood frame house in Boulder, Colorado. As a matter of fact, he was sleeping in the room which belonged to his mother when she was his age.

I'd just gotten to the part of the letter in which Dwight was describing the high school he was attending in Boulder when I became so sleepy. I couldn't believe how sleepy I was. Maybe I should ask for a cup of coffee instead of the hot chocolate? Maybe it was the fire in the fireplace, the warmth of the room, the coziness of the house, whatever. I was falling asleep while reading a letter I had waited months to receive.

I laid my head on the breakfast bar and closed my eyes.

I had a dream. My mother and father were alive again, but it wasn't like before. I was as old as I was now, and it looked as if my mom and dad had aged a bit, too.

They didn't live in their old house in the Bitterroot Valley. They had a new place, and they also had horses. I ran to the stables, and sure enough Tia and China were there. The two horses weren't fillies anymore. They were full-grown mares.

Dwight was in the stables. I couldn't believe my luck. Not only did my parents own horses, but somehow Dwight was there mucking out stalls.

I ran into the stall Dwight was working on. Dwight looked up from his work without a bit of recognition. When I hugged Dwight I could feel Dwight's body stiffen and react. He moved away from me.

"Let go of me!"

"Hug me back!" I blurted out, certain we were simply having

fun with one another.

Dwight was trying his best to get out of my grasp. I was stronger than Dwight remembered. Finally, we fell in the stall and were rolling around in the horse manure.

"John!"

It was my dad. He'd come into the barn.

"John, stop this foolishness right now!"

I let go of Dwight, who scrambled to his feet backing away from me. Maybe Dwight could see I was strong now, and didn't need a protector?

"He just came and grabbed me. I didn't have nothing to do with this!" Dwight protested.

In a flash my father was in the stall pulling me up. It hurt my arm the way he was dragging me out of the stables.

"What were you thinking, son?"

"Why doesn't Dwight know me, father?"

"That young black man just started work here today. We'll be lucky if he comes back after your little show."

We entered the back door of the house into the mud room.

"You strip out of those clothes. We'll need to get you into a shower."

I undressed and showered. What the hell did my father mean about Dwight being a hired hand? When I was drying myself off, my father returned.

"Just wrap the towel around you and come with me."

In the dream I followed my father down the hall. He opened a door and I stepped into a room which I recognized. It wasn't like it was my room, but it was certainly a young boy's room.

When father turned at the door I thought for a moment that my old man didn't really look like my old man, but he did look like someone I knew and trusted. I was puzzling over this when the man spoke up.

"You lay down on the bed. I'll be back later to help you get dressed," he said and then he closed and locked the door behind him.

I thought it was strange. Why would a fourteen-year-old boy need help dressing?

There was drool on the breakfast counter and drool on my face when I awakened. Dwight's letter was still open on the counter. I reached for the hot chocolate, but the cup was cold and the chocolate gone.

"Boy," Charles said from an armchair near the fireplace, "you must have been really tired."

"What time is it?"

"Time for us to get back to Rock Ranch."

"I didn't finish the letter."

"If you promise not to show it to anybody, you can take it with you."

I stacked the pages of the letter together, stuffed them in the envelope and grabbed my cowboy hat by the door.

On the ride back we loped up the horses almost the entire way. The back of my hair, which was long and draped over my collar, felt wet and cold in the freezing mountain air. I had a tendency to sweat a lot when I was sleeping.

That night after the horses had been put up, the stove stoked, and the horse work done, I got ready for bed.

As I took off my shirt I felt a pain in my right bicep. Going to the mirror I stared at the mark on my arm. It looked like the imprint of someone's large fingers.

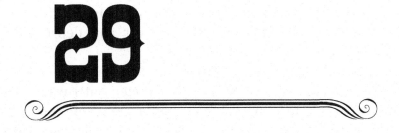

I was worried, but I didn't act like it. Something had happened in a dream and it had been reflected in the real world.

In world geography class we read about an African tribe that confused the real world with the dream world. In that African tribe if you insulted a member of the tribe in your dream it was expected that the next day you would go to that particular person and apologize. Everyone in the class had laughed about such a notion, but right now I didn't think it was so funny. Who was going to apologize to me for the mark on my arm?

I wasn't sure how it had happened, but I knew where it happened. It happened at Charles Dawson's house. I couldn't let Mr. Dawson know I knew.

Whenever Dawson came around I tried to act just like I'd acted before, but it wasn't easy. There was something creepy about him which I'd just now noticed. There was something in the way Dawson looked at me now which was different and I couldn't put my finger on it. And mostly, I just hoped the feeling would go away, and let me return to me and Charles being together.

After my last class I went to the administration building and into the outer office of the headmaster. His secretary, a stout woman in her sixties, who groaned whenever she stood up, was sitting behind her desk typing loudly on a report. She didn't look up until she wanted to.

"How can I help you?" she asked, not really sounding like she intended on helping at all.

"I was wondering if I could borrow the Polaroid?"

Without answering she reached over and depressed the lever on the intercom system.

"Headmaster, could you come out here, please?"

I didn't want to involve the headmaster, but I was in for a penny, so I was in for a pound. The headmaster came through his office door like he was ready to draw down on whoever was out there pestering him. But when he saw it was me his expression switched to a sort of smile.

"Well, come on, son," the headmaster said, ushering me into his office with a sweep of his hand.

I settled as best I could into the large brown leather chair opposite the desk. Surprisingly, the headmaster sat on the edge of his desk, and if I'd have wanted to I could have reached out and touched the headmaster's knee.

"You're the boy who lives in the stable, aren't you?"

"Yes sir, I'm John Wilson Barnes."

"You've done a fine job out there, really amazing. The way that place used to look and the way it looks now, it hardly seems to be the same place."

"Well, it's not the same place, sir."

The headmaster's eyes got big, then he burst out laughing. Sort of a machine gun laugh which drilled everything in the room, me included.

"What can I do for you, son?"

"I want to take pictures of the horses at the stables."

"So you want to borrow the Polaroid, do you?"

"Yes sir, I think it would be nice for the horses."

"What about Mr. Dawson, can he help you with that?"

"I'd like to surprise him, sir. And I'd like to surprise the horses."

"Do you think they care?"

"Yes sir, they're vain creatures, those horses."

Again the headmaster laughed, but this time it was like

report of a single rifle shot. It went right through my heart.

Headmaster got up, went around behind his desk. I could hear the scraping of a desk door. The headmaster pulled a Polaroid out and several cartridges of film.

"You know how this thing works?"

"Yes sir, my father had one."

"Good boy," headmaster said as he literally pushed me toward the closed door.

As I was leaving the outer office the headmaster spoke from his still opened door.

"If you get some good ones, we'll put them in the new brochure."

I was taking pictures of Tia and China. I had them in the large arena by themselves and I was cracking the buggy whip. It was making sharp reports in the afternoon air. Tia rolled her eyes in my direction and I cracked the whip again. Now, Tia and China were running in tandem like a team of working horses.

I dropped the buggy whip and pulled the Polaroid (which was around my neck) to eye level. After the first photo came out, I threw my hat down and tossed the still developing photos into the upside down crown of the hat. I did this each time the camera spit out a new photo.

"What ya doin', boy?" Dawson's voice was not friendly.

"Takin' pictures," was all I said, as I continued to throw the developing pictures into the crown of my hat.

"Who gave you permission to use the camera?" Charles asked, his voice a bit softer.

"Headmaster needs horse photos for the new brochure," I said, not wanting to sound like getting the camera was all my idea.

"There's gonna be a new brochure?" Charles asked in a rhetorical manner.

"That's what he says."

Dawson stood at the fence, one boot up on the bottom rail, his right arm resting on the top rung.

"If you're almost done, I can take the camera back for you. I'm going to the administration building now."

"Just getting started."

Much to my relief Charles stopped hanging on the fence and walked off toward the administration building. Sure Charles was going there for one reason and one reason only—to see if I had permission to use the camera.

That night with the door to the tack room locked and the fire built up, I spread the Polaroids of the horses on the bottom bunk. I'd taken some great shots even though it hadn't been my original intention.

My original intention I acted upon right now. I took off my shirt and stood in front of the small medicine cabinet mirror. I liked the way my stomach was flat and ridged just a little. I was in the greatest shape of my life, and the hard work had done it all.

I stood on my tip toes and held up my right arm, cocking it so the forearm lay across the top of my head. I got a fairly decent shot of the green and purple markings on the inside of my right bicep. I took several shots and laid them on the bunk. As they came into focus they showed quite nicely the hand-shaped bruise. I wasn't sure what I was going to do with those pictures, but I knew they needed to be taken before the bruise disappeared.

The Polaroids turned out great! It was perfectly clear, someone—not in a dream—had grabbed me and grabbed me hard! But who? And why? Obviously, it wasn't my father, he was dead. But maybe it was someone who I looked up to like a father? All these questions were simply a waste of time. Deep down I knew exactly whose handprint I had on the bicep of my right arm. It couldn't be anyone else. The man who had grabbed me and hurt me was Charles Alton Dawson. It happened the day at Dawson's house when I thought I'd fallen asleep at the breakfast bar. Something else had obviously happened. I didn't want to think about that.

Before this incident—it was the way I preferred to think of it, an incident—I'd trusted Charles Dawson, but now trust was out of the question.

I thought about showing the pictures to the headmaster, but something told me it probably wasn't a good idea. I realized I was at the bottom of a very large pecking order, or another more disturbing way to put it—I was at the bottom of a very large food chain.

Dwight had been the protector I needed; the protector I learned to love as a brother. I'd thought Mr. Dawson could possibly take Dwight's place, but that was absurd now. I needed a new protector and there wasn't another human at Rock Ranch whom I could trust. Wait a minute! Maybe I was needlessly limiting my search for protector. Maybe I was looking in the wrong species.

Santiago Sunrise, the horse I considered my very own, the

horse I was training to be my ride, perhaps Tia could look after me. It was a crazy idea! Tia was a yearling filly. True, she had joined up with me. She followed me, but how could I be sure she would, in fact, protect me? Was she even capable of caring for me in that way?

As I'd been wondering about Tia I drifted out to the barn area in the long double line of stalls. I walked down to the stall and stood outside the dutch door resting my elbows on the rail. China was asleep, lying in the far corner of the large stall. Tia came over and placed her big head on my left shoulder. Could she know what I was thinking? Could this be her way of saying, "Yes, I will protect you"?

Without thinking, I opened the stall door and stepped in beside Tia. I knew she couldn't be ridden, but I was a thin young man of fourteen and surely it couldn't hurt to get up on her? I laid my arms and upper body across where the saddle would go. Tia turned her head and looked at me with her left eye.

Slowly, I pulled myself up until I slipped my right leg over on the other side. My face was lying along the left side of her neck as she took a couple of uneasy steps.

"Easy girl. Easy."

Tia settled down and I sat up on her. It was at this precise moment that I saw the cowboy. The cowboy was seated on his paint. The cowboy's eyes were on me and I could have sworn the cowboy's paint was staring at Tia.

I started to speak but thought better of it. The cowboy smiled and patted his paint on the neck, then he began to stroke her there. I knew—I simply knew in my heart of hearts—the cowboy was telling me something about Tia without using words. Tia turned her head and looked at me. The love which flowed between the two of us filled my heart, and tears began to run down my cheeks. I felt this love and returned to resting my head on Tia's neck, and when I sat up and looked about, the stall was empty except for China, who was peacefully sleeping in her corner.

The next full school year was tough. I had decided not to show the photos to anyone and my arm returned to normal. But my trust of Charles Dawson was at an all-time low. There was only one problem. I couldn't let Charles know just how much I didn't trust him. Consequently, I walked a fine line never allowing myself to openly hate Mr. Dawson, but also never allowing myself to be alone with the man anywhere inside a building.

The upshot of all this meant I spent a whole lot of time with the horses and Charles. I had to admit Charles knew a lot about horses and I was adamant that I would learn what I could from the man without being alone with him.

Charles knew things had changed, but it was also obvious Charles wasn't quite sure what I knew. We played a game of balance.

At least once a week, and there are fifty-two of those in a year, Charles had asked me back out to his ranch. I always had an excuse. As a matter of fact I had filled a notebook full of excuses. Each was different and well thought out, but close to the end of the school year when I was getting ready to turn fifteen, Mr. Dawson confronted me with somewhat of an ultimatum and it ran like this.

We'd been working China and Tia in the round pen when Charles turned and said, "Wouldn't it be a shame if Rock Ranch decided to sell these fine young mares?"

I could tell this was bait so I didn't comment right away.

"Didn't you hear what I said?" Charles asked a bit annoyed.

"I heard," I said as I popped the buggy whip and got both Tia and China into a trot around the pen.

"And?" Charles said as he opened the gate, came in, closed it, and walked to the middle of the round pen where I was standing.

I lowered the whip and faced Charles.

"It would be a damn shame."

"They don't belong to you, you know?"

"I know, but sometimes I pretend they do."

"Pretending is a lie!" The way Charles said those words made me feel like he was talking about himself, not me.

I cracked the whip again and the girls picked up their pace.

"They could be yours. I could arrange it," Charles said in a softer tone.

"How could you do that?" Hell, I was interested. I really was, and for the first time in nearly a year Charles thought he might have the carrot he'd been looking for.

"What are you doing tonight?" Charles asked in a most nonchalant conversational tone.

"Thought I'd go over and watch some TV in the dorm rec room. I mean it's Friday night! Who wants to study?"

"Exactly," Charles said as he slapped me on the back. My bicep which hadn't hurt in a long time began to ache.

It was the first time Charles had intentionally touched me since I'd had that weird dream. I turned and looked at Charles. There was no smile on his face. There was no anger in his eyes, but somewhere in that particular glance I knew it was now or never.

"Come to my place. We'll take Tia and China out there, too," Charles said.

"And what's that going to accomplish?" I asked matter-of-factly, not even hinting I might be interested.

"You'll see," Charles said, then added without really thinking, "I still have a few tricks up my sleeve."

No kidding, I thought, then without even knowing I was going to say it added, "Sure, Charlie, let's do that."

Charles Dawson stood there without speaking.

Before he could speak I patted him on the arm.

"Let's go right after dinner. The daylight stays long this time of year," I said. Charles stood there while I walked to the stables.

As I was about to disappear around the corner of the stables Charles shouted out, "Don't worry. I'll put Tia and China back in the pasture."

33

I t would be hours before the sunset. Me and Charles made our way through the last of the Rock Ranch property to Mr. Charles Dawson's ranch. The clouds raced westward, but the surface winds were barely moving the limbs of the trees. Charles Dawson led the way. We were followed by Tia and China. I imagine his mind was racing in nearly every direction possible. This was the first time in nearly a year he'd been able to convince me to come to his ranch. I knew he'd convinced others to go out there, for he saddled horses for the other boys and they always looked like they'd been drugged upon their return.

I wasn't sure what I was going to do except I wasn't going to have myself go unconscious and have a repeat of whatever happened nearly a year ago. My plans were fuzzy, but my resolve was firm. One way or the other, I was through dodging Mr. Charles Dawson. I was through worrying about a man who essentially meant nothing to me.

We rode the horses into the paddock area and Charles dismounted. Tia and China had followed us across the road, but only Tia had gone right into the fenced in area. I rode out and corralled China back to where she should be.

"Come on girl." I clicked my tongue and rode up behind her.

China also entered the paddock area and Charles closed the gate behind them. He began taking the saddle off his horse.

I stayed mounted.

"Aren't you going to take the saddle off your horse and let him rest a bit?" Charles asked.

"He can rest with his saddle on," I replied as I dismounted, "I'll loosen the latigo and leave it at that."

The ranch house was warm and cozy just like it been the previous times I'd been there. Perhaps, it was my heightened awareness which made me wonder why anyone, not just Charles Dawson, would build a fire up if they hadn't planned on being back to the home. There was really only one answer; something was in the works.

To allow Charles to do whatever it was he was planning, I excused myself to use the bathroom. I walked down the hall, turned on the bathroom light, and shut the door with a slam! Then I ducked into Charles master bedroom. I could hear Charles come to the edge of the hall. I pictured him looking down the hall and seeing the bathroom door shut and the light under the door. I heard him slip away from the hallway entrance.

I saw Charles hurry into the kitchen. Tiptoeing down the hall, I laid myself against the wall closest to the kitchen. Carefully, I peeked around the corner just in time to see Charles pull a medicine bottle down from the cabinet. He took the cap off and shook several drops into a glass of Pepsi. He then slid the Pepsi over to where I would be sitting. He started to put the medicine bottle back, but thought better of it. He took the cap off and for good measure shook several more drops into the glass.

I tiptoed back down the hall and slipped into the bathroom. Flushing the toilet, I washed my hands twice and looked into the mirror.

"No matter what happens, I'm going to be OK," I said to myself. Then again, in a whisper, "No matter what happens, I'm going to be OK." I don't know if I believed this because my mouth was like cotton, and I couldn't have spit on a bet. But mustering my cowboy courage and screwing it in place, I thought, *that man would piss on your leg and tell you it's raining.*

34

He was sitting at the breakfast bar when I emerged from the hallway. "Thought you might like a Pepsi?"

"You must be reading my mind, I'm about to die of thirst," I said, inwardly smiling to myself.

I pulled out the barstool in front of my drink and sat down.

Charles could not keep himself from smiling. Ten minutes after I drank the soda the fun would begin.

I picked up my glass and raised it to my lips. His creepy eyes followed the glass as it got closer to my mouth. Suddenly, I lowered the glass. The smile disappeared.

"You know," I said as a matter-of-fact, "I'd enjoy the Pepsi more, if we had some chips."

"Of course, some chips, how thoughtless of me," Charles jumped up opened the cabinet above the stove to retrieve a bag of chips.

I'd seen this done in a thousand movies. You simply switched the glasses and acted as if you'd done nothing. Charles poured the chips into a bowl and placed them between the two drinks. I took a handful of chips, gobbled them down, then picked up the Pepsi and slaked my thirst with half of the drink.

Charles laughed out loud and did the same with a handful of chips, then to encourage me he drained his now poisoned glass of Pepsi in several quick gulps.

"Do you want some more Pepsi?" I asked as I got up and went to the refrigerator. I took the Pepsi bottle out and poured more into Charles's glass. I drank down the other half of my glass and added more there, too.

"I was thirstier than I thought!"

Both Charles and I burst into laughter, he not realizing both of us were laughing for the same reason. I didn't plan it that way, but that's the way it turned out. We were sitting there talking, mostly small talk. Charles poured us a bit more Pepsi and shook a few more chips into the bowl.

Fairly soon, Charles started glancing at the kitchen clock which was shaped like a black cat whose eyes swung in tandem with the cattail pendulum below. That clock reminded me of the nice woman who had kept me for a while after I'd been arrested. Charles looked at the kitchen clock, then glanced at his wristwatch. At one point, Charles wiped his face with both hands, then looked at his hands is if they weren't quite his own. Magically Charles knew he'd drunk the drugged Pepsi. He knew it, but his perverted mind would not accept it. He had decided he was going to drug this young man and have his way with him. Perhaps, it was the anticipation of the excitement he would enjoy which kept him in denial about what was really happening. When Charles's jaw dropped open and he seemed unable to close it, I got up.

"Where... are... you going?" Charles asked, barely able to finish the sentence.

"Well," I said, striking a pose like the cowboy I so admired, my thumbs tucked into each of my jean pockets, "I guess I'm gonna go just about wherever I want to go, Mr. Charles Dawson, child molester!"

Dawson's eyes grew large with fear. He tried getting up, but his legs fumbled with the railing on the stool. He managed to untangle them just long enough to take a few sliding steps before he tripped and fell badly. He went down on his face and wasn't able to put his hands up to protect himself. His face bounced off the Mexican tiles. It was one sweet face plant!

"Whoa! I'll bet that hurt!" I said as I walked closer to where Charles had sprawled out.

"You're... gonna... be sorry," was all Charles could get out as he tried desperately to get up. He grabbed a hold of one of the dining room chairs and tried to pull himself up. He almost managed to get up before the chair slipped on the Mexican tiles and he and the chair clattered to the floor.

I knelt down a safe distance from where Charles was laid out on his back.

"Do I have to wait to be sorry? Hell, I'm already sorry, Charlie. Sorry you ever came to work at Rock Ranch. Sorry you thought you could drug me and have your way with me."

"I never—" was all Charles could say before he completely passed out.

I walked over to his spread eagle body.

"A part of me wants to hurt you, but that would be too much like you. So, I'm leaving, hoping never, ever to see you or your kind again."

Back outside I had raided his kitchen cabinets and had grocery bags full of canned goods. I packed the cans and other supplies into two duffel bags. Tia was tied to the fence and I placed a sawbuck saddle I'd found in Charles' barn on her. I lifted one of the duffel bags and secured it with a barrel hitch onto the sawbuck saddle. I hurriedly stuffed canned goods in the other duffel bag until it was about as full as the first one. I hoisted this duffel bag up and secured it to the other side of the sawbuck saddle with another barrel hitch.

Back in the house I ran around opening every drawer I could find and pitching what I thought I might need in the middle of the living room.

At one point, I walked over to Charles and nudged him with my boot. Charles was still out like a light. I ran to the bedroom and found a pistol in the nightstand. It was a 380 Starr Modella, a Spanish automatic. I pushed the release and checked to make sure it was loaded. It was! I racked the slide and a round jumped out! There had been one in the chamber. I pushed that round back into the clip, shoved the clip in place, and racked the same shell back into the chamber. I flicked the safety on and pushed the Spanish 380 into the front of my jeans. It felt good there, like nothing would ever happen again that was bad to me. Reaching deep into the nightstand drawer I pulled a box of one hundred 380 shells from the drawer. I also discovered a silver Zippo lighter which I opened. I snaked the flint with the striker and a flame jumped up in its corrugated cage. I closed the lighter on my pants and put it in my pocket.

Opening the next drawer down on the nightstand, I found a bundle of letters. They were tied together with string. Immediately, I recognized Dwight's handwriting. So, he had written after all, and now I had the letters which Charles had tried to keep from me. I stuffed the letters into my back pocket. I ran from the house with two pillow cases full of stuff. I entered the paddock area and finished placing those items in the duffel bags.

"I'm sorry about this girl, but you're going to have to be our pack horse. I think you're stronger than China, that's why I chose you."

I took the rein from the hackamore which Tia was wearing and tied it to one of the rear D rings on my saddle.

Tia flicked her ears suddenly and out of the corner of my eye I caught a movement, I jerked away from the movement as a piece of firewood glanced off the side of my cowboy hat knocking it to the ground.

Charles Dawson had swung that hefty piece of firewood hoping to put me totally out of commission. The centripetal force from the swing pulled Charles off balance and he fell in the mud.

Sputtering, trying to regain his feet, Charles began screaming. "You no good son of a bitch! You bastard! I'm going to kill you!"

I truly believed Charles would do exactly what he said he would do.

The blood from his broken nose had dried on his face, giving him the look of an Indian on the warpath. He got back on his feet and took a couple of practice swings with the firewood.

"I'm gonna knock this one right out of the park!"

I drew the Spanish 380 and released the safety.

"That's my gun!" Charles shouted, and took a step in my direction as my trigger finger tightened. Then, without warning, Tia bucked and kicked. Cans went flying from one of the duffel bags. I saw one of her hooves make contact with the side of Charles Dawson's head. Charles dropped to the ground like a sack of rocks.

I put the safety back on and tucked the automatic away. I went to Charles Dawson's side. Blood was running from both of his ears and from his mouth and nose.

Tia came over and smelled the downed man.

"I think we killed him, girl!"

Tia snorted twice as if she understood.

"Mister," I said, already depersonalizing the body lying in the paddock area, one leg bent oddly beneath it, its head twisted awkwardly to the side, "if you hadn't been what you are and done what you did, this never woulda happened."

I looked around. I was sure someone had witnessed the killing of Charles Dawson. Then, I saw them. The sangha of trees were watching wordlessly. The tall pines with their skinny trucks swayed leisurely in the breeze which had kicked up, and the quivers shook their two-sided leaves to applaud what had happened. It was a different sangha of trees than the ones I'd depended upon when I first got to Rock Ranch, but in essence, it was the same mother nature who saw everything and missed nothing.

"He brought it on himself," I shouted to the gathering of trees hoping they would understand. The wind died immediately, and all was quiet, as was the man in the paddock area.

Tia turned away from the fallen man as if she'd seen and heard enough. A few minutes later both Tia and China were in a line behind me as I mounted the roan. I took one final look at the inert body of Charles Dawson.

"See you Charles. Maybe on the other side."

35

The breeze was wonderful. It was full of pine and wildflower smells. The meadows were brilliant emerald green mixed with so many other colors and hues I wasn't sure I'd ever seen the world so crystal clear and serene. A dead man, who brought it all on himself, lay in the paddock area of his ranch. This really should have upset me more than it did. At least I hadn't had to shoot him.

The Spanish 380, the Starr Modelo, fit nicely in my hand and I knew how to use it. Center mass. I would have shot Charles. What kind of man would drug a child and have his way with him? The bullet would have gone through Charles's black heart and gone out his back. I was glad I didn't have to shoot. Glad the killing bullet hadn't exited Charles body and done harm to one of the horses. Glad Tia had stepped in and ended it all.

I had the distinct impression she'd done it to protect me, but maybe she'd bucked and kicked because of the sawbuck saddle. She'd never, ever had any sort of saddle on her. Perhaps she was simply trying to buck off the saddle. And perhaps not!

I reached out with my left hand and touched Tia's nose as she plodded behind the Roan.

"Good girl," I said, and then I was struck by the kindness in those deep brown eyes. Tears welled up. "I love you, girl," I said, then corrected myself by spreading my arms wide. "I love all you horses!"

That evening late—the sun doesn't set in Montana till after ten at night during the summer months—I made a camp back in the recess of a hill. The wind, which was from the west, slipped over the little cave and barely disturbed the fire I'd made.

All in all I'd done a fine job packing. I had to thank Conrad and his dog, Johnny-Boy, for that. The months I'd spent up in the Sapphires with those two and all the sheep had taught me what a man needed to do to survive.

The bacon was sizzling nicely in the pan, and as it grew crisp I drained the grease then threw a can of pinto beans in on top. When the mess of beans and bacon bubbled, I took it off the fire and ate it using slices of white bread like tortillas.

I hobbled all three horses in a stand of quivers—other people called them aspens—but the sheepherder called them quivers and to me that name made sense. Quivers they were and always would be. The camp was nearly hidden, but I worried a little about the prophesied pumas and grizzlies always touted as the last defense against fleeing boys. Sleep overcame my worry and I didn't awaken until first light.

As I prepared breakfast I wasn't sure when the other foremen at Rock Ranch would start to look for me. First, they would have to miss me which wouldn't be easy under the circumstances. Hardly anyone came out to the barn and stables and thinking about it again I was almost sure they'd miss Mr. Charles Dawson before they'd miss me.

I felt bad about the horses I'd left behind—Randy, Chris, Rusty, Lucy, Blondie—all of them would wonder where I was, or more accurately, they would wonder where their hay was.

I made up my mind; those horses, that barn, that stable, that tack room turned bedroom were all things of the past and they must remain that way.

There was no going back.

Sipping on my third cup of black cowboy coffee, I remembered Dwight's letters. I took them from his saddle bags and read all seven of them as my morning fire died to embers. It was a great feeling for me to read all about Dwight's new life. He liked living with his grandparents in Boulder, Colorado and in his last letter Dwight even admitted he had a college girlfriend who thought Dwight was in college, too. Our two lives couldn't be any different. Dwight in a serene home environment, enjoying his normal life; Me once again a fugitive at large, and this time I wasn't simply a horse thief, this time I was a murderer. This time when the police showed up, they'd shoot first and ask questions later.

For these reasons and more, I decided to stay away from any populated area. I would drive the horses north and go deep into the woods. Good thing it was the beginning of summer. The daylight would burn late into the night and allow me time to flee. Of course, that meant those looking for me would have a similar advantage.

I knew that moss grew on the trees heaviest on the north side, away from the sun, so I followed the heavy moss growth north.

Halfway through the first full day I watered the horses at a crystal-clear stream. I knew Montana geography fairly well and I travelled as best I could navigating north by northwest. I figured I was headed toward the Rocky Mountain Range and the Continental Divide. Going higher this early in the summer would mean I might run into colder weather, possibly even some snow. Good thing I'd taken the coat, gloves, and muffler off the hat tree just inside that man's front door. I couldn't say his name; I couldn't even think his name. He would remain *that man* from now on.

I was beginning to feel badly about that man. Not because that man deserved these feelings, but more because all people were children at one time and surely that man hadn't started out as a sexual predator. More than likely, he'd been molested when he was a kid and confused the betrayal of adults and their lustful ways with the warm, fuzzy feelings of being loved.

After watering the animals, I decided to take a nap. Yes, I could've slept in the saddle, but I didn't have a night latch on my saddle horn. I could have devised a night latch, but the problem was without a clearly marked trail I couldn't be sure the horses would continue on the truly northern trek. I hobbled all the horses in a small meadow near a crystal, clear stream. They could eat their fill of the sweet grass and I could escape into sleep. Unfortunately, sometimes, sleep brings other things than restfulness.

36

When I awakened it was already too late. I never knew so many of the kids from Rock Ranch could ride. All the horses I knew by name; Chris, Rusty, Lucy & Blondie. They were all there. Some were being ridden by foreman, some by the kids. The obvious leader of the make-shift posse was Charles Alton Dawson himself. Yeah, I know, I wasn't going to say, or even think, his name again, but there he was in the flesh.

Charles's smile was ruined by the bandages on his face. Blood still trickled down beneath the white tape holding the bandages on.

Charles threw a giant loop from his saddle rope and caught me as I tried to run toward the hobbled horses. I'd left the Roan's saddle loose. One quick pull, a kick in the Roan's stomach, one more pull on the latigo, and I'd be up and riding again.

But the rope caught me along the left shoulder and under the right armpit.

Charles brought his horse to a quick stop and I went down on my butt. Cheers went up from the men, boys, and even the horses that encircled me. Strange, I'd never heard cheering horses before.

Everyone grinned maniacally, but no one was saying a word. The only sound was the heavy breathing of the horses. They must have ridden hard throughout the night.

The sun was barely up, and a low mist hung over the tiny meadow. It looked as if my three horses were legless, their bodies floating on the mist.

Charles had dropped down off his horse and tightened the cinch on the Roan just as I'd wanted to do in making my getaway.

A hangman's rope, complete with the thirteen knots of the hangman's noose, was thrown to Charles by someone, I couldn't tell who. Wait a minute; it was one of the first kids who had bullied me when I arrived at Rock Ranch. That figured.

Before I could protest, my hands were tied behind my back, the noose placed over my head and tightened, and I was hoisted up on the back of the Roan. I tried to place boot toes through the stirrups, but Charles took a small lead of rope and tied the stirrups together underneath the Roan. I guessed where I was going I wouldn't need the stirrups, after all.

The end of the hanging rope was thrown over a branch of a Live Oak tree and tied about the gnarly trunk.

The horses lined up in a circle around the hanging tree. Why wasn't someone saying something? This muted death bothered me!

Charles raised his hand, smiled a bloody psychotic smile and slapped the Roan's haunches.

The Roan shot forward and even though I didn't especially want to go on this particular ride, I was on my way. The rope tugged at my neck and I was jerked from the saddle.

At that precise moment everything stopped. The men on horses stiffened like statues in a park. The menacing faces and shouts of hatred were frozen, mouths open mid-yell.

From the nearby meadow where Tia and China grazed came a lone rider. At first, I wasn't sure who it was, but then, who else could it be?

It was the cowboy. He was smiling and walking his magnificent horse toward the dreadful scene. The cowboy whoaed his horse right beside me.

"How are you today?" he asked in his wonderful mellow voice. The rope was tugging slightly on my neck.

"I've had better days, but if this is what it takes to see you and talk with you I'd have to say it's a good day."

The cowboy's smile broadened, his white teeth sparkling behind his tanned face.

"I have to say, son, the one thing which has always amazed me concerning you is your ability to see good everywhere and be grateful for it."

"Thank you, sir."

"I rest my case."

"Will I be joining you now I'm about to die?"

The cowboy looked at me quizzically, like a dog tilts its head at a high pitched sound. "You have always been with me, John, as I have always been with you. Why do you think you've seen me so many times?"

"I thought I was lucky, I guess."

"*Blessed* is the word you're looking for. Others look for me in the books concerning the Old West, but if they'd really pay attention they would have noticed me. Most who see me aren't reading about me when it happens. I'm not in the books. I'm in the world."

"Who are you really? You're not simply a cowboy, are you?"

"There are clues to my true identity, but really, who cares who I really am? The point is you were with me, John Wilson Barnes, before you were born, you are with me now. And you will be with me after you pass from this world which I so love."

"Thank you."

"By the way, I have appeared to you now in this horrific dream—"

"This is only a dream?"

"As is most of life."

"But I mean this," I gestured widely. "All this is simply a dream?"

"It is!"

"Thank God!"

"You're welcome. And yet... leaving as you think you are

now... this leaving may, in the ways of the world, be easier than what is ahead of you."

"You know what is ahead of me?"

"I know some, I can guess the rest. I'm a pretty good guesser. Anyway, the Prince of the Air will soon be saddling up next to you. You will be tested. You will be tried—as all those who truly love me are."

"How will I get through these tests, sir?"

"As you always have. With one ear toward the world which I so love, and the other ear you must attune to me." The Cowboy reached out and placed his hand on my head in blessing, and then he slid his big brown hand down my face closing my eyes.

"I am with you even to the end of the world," was the last thing I heard before I woke up.

It was a weird dream, to be sure. It seemed the cowboy was God. That was crazy. The cowboy was a cowboy. I guessed in my confused state of mind (after all, I'd just killed someone and was on the run from the law), in my confused state of mind, I could imagine almost anything. I shook off the dream, saddled up, and with Tia and China following, rode north again.

I followed Highway 89 past Freezeout Lake. Just before the town of Choteau I saw the map symbol for an unpaved road. That road went directly west then north by northwest leading to the base of Teton Peak.

The cars traveling between Great Falls and Choteau paid me little mind. At fifteen years of age and my cowboy hat pulled down snug I could easily be mistaken for a ranch hand or trail guide. Anywhere else but Montana it might seem strange to see a man riding a Roan toward the mountains with a pack horse and a spare horse, but not here in big sky country.

Just before the cutoff on Highway 89 I heard a car come up from behind and slow down. I was well off on the right shoulder, posing no problem to traffic in either direction. I wanted to look and see who it was, but thought better of it. After being followed for nearly a mile with other cars passing the slower vehicle and moving on, there was a short burst of siren—a whoop-whoop—I turned to my left in the saddle. There on the side of the car following me were the words: Teton County Sheriff's Department.

The Sheriff's deputy had the passenger side window down

and he shouted through it.

"You ain't from around here, are you son?" the Sheriff's deputy asked.

"No sir, I'm not," I answered, neither stopping nor going any faster.

"Where you headed?"

"Up toward Teton Peak," I answered still turned in the saddle.

"Looks like you're fixin' to stay a piece," the officer noted.

"Yes sir, that's a fact," came my reply.

"Goin' huntin'?"

"Well, I sure ain't runnin' away from home," I said casually.

"A boy was reported escaped from Rock Ranch. You seen any boys on this road?"

My heart was in his throat. The officer certainly wouldn't be asking me about myself, plus, it was obvious no one at Rock Ranch knew about that man's death or the missing horses.

"How old a boy we talking about?" I managed to ask trying to keep my voice down in my throat.

"Not sure. Somewhere between the ages of ten to fifteen," the deputy answered.

"It's just been me, the horses, and the cars whizzing by," I said with as much finality as I could muster.

A crackling sound and garbled words came from the radio in the Sheriff's deputy's car. I couldn't make out what was being said.

The Sheriff's deputy listened, then hollered up to me.

"There's been a wreck, a car wreck, down to Fairfield. Good luck hunting, son!"

"Thanks," I said as I waved goodbye.

The deputy whooped his siren in reply, twisted his steering wheel, and mashed on the gas pedal. The car spun around nicely and I could hear the four barrel carburetor suck air as he sped down the highway away from me.

I patted the Roan on the side of the neck. He'd spooked a little when the gravel had been thrown up by the retreating deputy's car, but had quickly settled down.

"Well, fellow travellers, it looks like the Cowboy is still with us," I said to the horses. I kicked the Roan into a trot and the string of horses, Tia and China, responded in kind.

It would always, always, be remembered as the best summer of my short life. Up around the three-thousand foot level of Teton Peak I found what could only be described as the perfect camping meadow. The meadow was green from the spring runoff and wild flowers were everywhere. One section had wild mustard growing in it and each time the horses grazed there they returned with yellow muzzles.

I laughed when I saw the yellow faces, and it made me think of a time when I'd returned to my parents covered in pollen and my father had called me "number one son!" I laughed to myself remembering that day, and then I laughed no more when I recollected being taken from the church which was pregnant with the corpses of my parents. I had been misunderstood that day. Misunderstood and chastised. It would have been easy for me to get bitter from the multitude of times I'd done one thing and everyone had thought I'd done something entirely different.

Conrad, the sheepherder with Johnny-Boy at his side had told me many stories the summer I was with them, as we sat around the campfire. Conrad had read a lot and told me that certain Japanese Buddhists believe it was possible to live a life of one continuous mistake. It seemed those particular Japanese believed this life of one continuous mistake was also an enlightened life.

I wasn't sure what *enlightened* meant, but I was sure it had something to do with being on a high mountain plateau and being content with whatever came your way.

That summer I built a round pen out of deadfall and each day for three to four hours I did ground work with Tia and China.

Dwight was going to be surprised at what a wonderfully

trained horse China was. I knew, yes, I knew, I really knew, on some level me and Dwight would someday be reunited. I wanted to talk to the Cowboy about it, but since that last dream I hadn't actually seen the Cowboy. Naturally, I felt close to the Cowboy when working with Tia and China and of course, I felt the Cowboy's presence most keenly when mounted on the Roan.

Once in a while when I heard gunshots, whether hunters or someone simply practicing their aim, and I got scared that the Teton County Sheriff's Department had mounted an assault like the one I'd experienced when Conrad had turned me in. But it was usually just shots in the distance without the follow-up of four-wheel vehicles, unwanted law enforcement, and air support helicopters.

My life was as exciting as any book I'd read and I swore that someday I'd try to put on paper some of what had come my way.

Mariah was asleep on the big comfortable chair in my hospital room. I didn't know how long she'd been that way. I took a look at the miniature tape recorder; the red light was still on, and I guessed it was still working, but I was so disconnected from technology I simply pushed the stop button. The recorder clicked loudly and Mariah stirred in her chair.

"I'm so sorry, grandpa, I must have fallen asleep."

"It's okay, darlin', but I'm just not sure there's any tape left in the recorder."

"It's digital, grandpa, there's no tape."

"No tape, then how? Never mind, even if you explained it to me, I wouldn't understand."

I laughed softly, and Mariah joined in.

"I'm awake now. Go on with the story."

"You sure?"

She reached over and took my gnarled hand in hers. "I'm feeling I'm getting to know you for the first time. Go on." She pushed the record button again.

So go on I did.

The canned goods I'd taken from that man's ranch had almost ran out by the time it was mid-July, but Conrad had shown me many edible greens which, when cooked right, were full of nutrition and didn't taste too bad.

If I could have done anything different when I made my escape from that man's ranch I would have located a rifle.

It wasn't that I was a bad shot with the little automatic. I was a good shot with the Starr Modelo 380, but the range of the pistol was only about 100 feet. I'd managed to sneak up on several rabbits, but what I wanted was venison, elk, or even bear.

I got real tired of eating rabbit. I'd shot one; merely wounding it and had to wring its neck. The rabbit squealed horribly and it put me off my appetite for rabbit for a bit.

I'd gone with my father when he'd hunted deer and I finally decided to use one of my father's methods in order to get a deer. Father had taken deer antlers and knocked them together. You don't have to hunt the deer, then, they simply came to where you were.

I'd found an old skeleton of a deer. The coyotes and bear had drug off major portions of the carcass when it still had meat on it, but nothing had disturbed the fine rack of antlers which were still attached to its skull.

I broke the skull in half with a large rock thereby separating the large rack into two halves then found a growth of Ponderosa Pines. Moving in between the trees, I situated myself on a large pile of dried pine needles, well hidden from the meadow. I rattled the broken rack the way I'd seen my father do it.

I sat most of the morning knocking those antlers together. Tia, China, and the Roan watched the grove of pines at first, but after half an hour or so, and they became accustomed to the sound and paid no more attention.

Sometime in the afternoon—I wasn't sure exactly what time since my only watch was the sun—I grew weary of knocking the antlers together. No deer had come. I hadn't even seen a deer at the end of a long meadow. Perhaps it was the wrong time of year for attracting deer like that. Whatever! I gave up and crawled from beneath the Ponderosas.

Then, quite unexpectedly, I saw movement out of the corner of my left eye. I turned to see a puma! He was perched on a ledge behind the grove of trees. He was less than twenty feet away from where I stood.

The movement I'd seen was the swishing of the puma's tail. I knew what that meant. The puma had locked in. While I'd been hunting deer, the puma had been hunting me!

I unbuttoned my shirt, grabbed a shirttail in each hand and raised the shirt above my head. I'd heard old timers talking about ways to scare off a mountain lion. This method was supposed to make me about twice as large as I first appeared.

The puma's tail just kept on twitching. The mountain lion had locked in and he wasn't going to let something like a shirt scare him away.

I knew better than to fall down in a fetal position and cover my head with my arms. The puma would shred my arms in order to get at my head. I also knew better than to run. If I ran the big cat would be on me, biting the large vein in my neck and tearing open my chest with his powerful claws. Besides, beyond me and further into the meadow were my three horses. Hobbled as they were they would be easy targets for the cat who might kill all three horses just for the sport of it.

I yelled. The cat's tail swished. Slowly, I took the Starr

Modelo 380 from my Wranglers. I didn't want to make any quick movements which would entice the cat to pounce.

I raised the little automatic up and aimed right between the cat's eyes. It was such a beautiful specimen—how could I kill it? Then, the cat growled, low and menacing.

My first shot went wide right. A branch behind and to the left of the big cat exploded causing the cat to leap.

It was true. I knew it now. When an emergency happened things move quite slowly.

I saw the first rapid steps of the big cat, but I did not see the cat jump. What I did do was not close my eyes. With the cat in the air it couldn't exactly move.

I pulled the trigger six times before the cat hit me. The cat weighed in around one hundred twenty pounds and that weight traveling through the air knocked me down and knocked the breath right out of me. I was down with the cat lying on top of me. I wanted to move, but first I had to catch my breath.

My first big intake of breath almost choked me. The acrid smell of the big cat filled my lungs. I pushed hard on the puma and rolled to my right jumping up and aiming the automatic at the inert form of the animal.

I had two shots left. I'd counted—the one wide right and the six shots at the cat in midair. There were nine rounds in the 380. One in the chute and eight in the clip. I'd fired seven so there were two left—one in the chamber and one in the clip.

The cat didn't move. Not one single bit. A pool of blood formed under it, visible as it pooled out away from the cat's body.

I built up the embers of last night's fire. I really got it roaring, burning the large logs down nicely with big, glowing embers. I arranged a spit over the intense heat and placed the skewer through the neck of the puma and out through the ass end. I wasn't sure how long I'd have to rotate the animal, but—as my father once said—what was time to a pig?

The rotating and roasting flesh of the puma smelled good. It didn't smell like beef, chicken, rabbit, venison, or wild bird. I guessed it smelled exactly like a roasting puma.

I pulled a small strip of meat from the outside of the cat. After blowing on it, I popped it on into my mouth. My mouth answered by squirting generous amounts of saliva over the cooling meat. It tasted... good, real good! I chewed greedily on the freshly roasted puma.

Who knew cat meat was good meat!?

I ate as much as I could. Too much, really. It tasted so good. When the fire burned down and I no longer had to turn the meat, I fell asleep.

When I woke up, the portion of the cat closest to the coals had burned badly, but the upper portion was still good.

Again, at dinner, I ate as much of the meat as I could. There was no way which I knew to preserve the rest of the meat. I would be generous and share it with the coyotes.

I dragged what was left of the puma to the edge of a cliff which bordered one side of the mountain meadow. I pushed the warm meat off the cliff and watched it as a broke apart and scattered.

That night I woke from what I thought was a bad dream, but was only the sound of growling coyotes tearing apart what was left of the big cat. I smiled to myself and said out loud, "Thank you, Cowboy."

40

When I lived with Conrad and Johnny-boy I helped Conrad cure the hide of a dead sheep which had been attacked one night by a wolf. The wolf had simply broken the sheep's neck and gnawed on it after it was killed.

Conrad said he cured the pelts of animals the way a Native American friend had taught him—the old-fashioned way. He used the animal's brain and rubbed it on the inner side of the pelt. Something in the brain kept the hide part of the pelt from rotting. It was a stinking business, usually accompanied by literally thousands of flies. Conrad had encouraged me not to shoo the flies away. Conrad wasn't sure, but he thought the flies feasting on the rubbed-in brain matter might also help the curing process. Once a pelt was entirely covered by the brain matter, the hide was stretched on a hoop made of willow sticks woven together in a circle and then allowed to dry. If done right, the pelt was soft and pliable. If done wrong the skin would harden and resist being folded by breaking into sections.

A week after I killed the puma I went to check on the hide.

I'd used a lasso to string the pelt into a tall tree, hoping it would keep varmints away and allow the pelt to cure without being disturbed.

Big cumulonimbus clouds were piling up south of my location. The puffy, pillow-like monster clouds formed often when the weather was hot and the days were long. I wasn't even sure what month it was, forget about what day it was. I knew it was summer because summer was the only time Montana got hot.

Days had been long and hot with the sun setting way into the evening. I remembered from the clock in the tack room during the height of summer the sun wouldn't go down until around ten. I supposed it was precisely this time of year I was dealing with now.

The breeze coming up the mountain smiled into my green meadow and Tia and China were especially excitable this day. They ran and bucked and farted, playing what could only be supposed as some form of equine tag.

Tia's mane, all golden and silky, was flying out from her head and neck. She held her tail out straight behind her and its length easily equaled half her body. Seeing her run with the darker China—her mane and tail doing a good imitation of Tia's—stirred something in my heart.

The way I felt was odd, though. With the warm breeze in my face, the smell of the heated Ponderosas filling my flared nostrils, and the sight of the two animals I loved best running like the very wind, all those things combined to fill me with a feeling I usually only had when the Cowboy appeared.

The feeling lifted me up and I felt like a god myself. It seemed like it would be the perfect time to simply stop living.

For the first time in my life I realized the Cowboy was truly everywhere and in everything. From the dirt which spilled from the horses hooves to the most spacious, light-filled sunrise, it was all good—all Cowboy.

I couldn't figure out why cats didn't like the rain. When I still lived with my parents, our next door neighbor had seven cats. They would lay about the yards scratching, yawning, playing with string, licking themselves, when all of the sudden it would start to rain. The cats would scatter like roaches in the kitchen when you turned on the light.

That's what I was having trouble figuring out. Why would they run from the storm like it was raining sulfuric acid? These thoughts came to me as I sat by my campfire in the rain. The rain had put the fire out twenty minutes ago, yet I sat there perfectly dry under the newly cured puma pelt.

I wore the pelt with the big cat's head covering my own head. The ears of the puma (which could no longer hear) perched now on top of my head. Wrapped in the length of the big cat I was perfectly dry. Perfectly dry! So why was it cats didn't like the rain?

Tia and China were standing in the corner of the meadow close to where I sat motionless. They didn't seem to mind the rain. The Roan stood nearby, also not bothered by the downpour. The Roan's left rear leg was cocked a bit and that hoof was balanced on its front tip. I knew from taking care of the horses at Rock Ranch many of them slept in that particular manner—either the left or right rear leg cocked and the front feet flat on the ground.

Odd. Thinking about Rock Ranch made me homesick for the place. Not the "after-Dwight-Rock-Ranch" when that man, the pervert, had showed up, but the Rock Ranch with me and Dwight snuggled into our bunk beds, the fire glowing low in the potbellied stove and the sound of our voices low and respectful as we talked about life, love, girls, horses and getting back to the real world. I missed that Rock Ranch. I would have gladly stayed there till I turned eighteen, but knew I was only dreaming. Wishful thinking is what they called that. Daydreaming was another name for it. And those two forms of thinking always seemed to center on the past.

I needed to start planning for the future. But what sort of future does a fifteen-year-old boy have as a murderer and a horse thief? That's what you call a rhetorical question. For there was only one possible answer. If caught—and something told me I was bound to be at some point—when caught was more like it. When caught the only future for John Wilson Barnes was a lifetime behind bars.

I shivered in the warm summer rain even though I wasn't cold. Really, I began to sweat under the waterproof hide. No, the future was not bright. I wished I could blame my mom and dad, but seriously, all they'd done was die in a car wreck. A morbid part of me now wished I'd died with them. But looking up at the Roan, Tia, and China I understood I never would have come to know these magnificent horses, nor the Cowboy, Himself, if it hadn't happened. If my father and mother hadn't died none of this would have happened. Then, inside me, I heard an old hymn from the clapboard church back in the Bitterroot. "Joyful... Joyful, we adore thee!" the first line went. Yes, it was joyful to know and adore, but did that mean I was glad my parents were dead? Holding my knees I hummed the hymn and rocked back and forth in the rain.

Some things simply can't be understood, or more precisely, some things *can't* be simply understood.

41

S ummer was coming to an end. The leaves had not begun to change colors yet, but when the wind blew high in the Ponderosa Pines the whistling sounded colder.

I realized I was using more firewood in my morning fire and sitting beside the fire for longer periods of time.

I managed to wash my clothes in a nearby brook. I used sand on my clothes the way Conrad had shown me. My white underwear was dingy grey, but my shirt and jeans didn't look too bad. Now I wished I'd taken clothes from that man's ranch. They would have been too big—just a little—but it would have given me a variety of things to wear. My Wranglers were wearing thin and there was already a hole in the left elbow of my only shirt.

Food was exceptionally low, but the horses continued to feast on the tall sweet grass. Tia, China, and the Roan had grown fat and sassy. I'd planned to train the horses on a more regular schedule, but somehow the actual practice of it had gotten away from me.

During the summer heat I heard shots and supposed they were poachers or people practicing their aim. I'd also seen some campers from afar, but had kept my distance being a murderer and all.

This particular day I was sitting in the forested area nearest to my high meadow camp. I'd taken to sitting quietly in the forest. As such, animals of all types—squirrels, rabbits, rock badgers, deer and even a bear or two—had wandered very close to where I was seated without noticing.

At first I thought I'd use this ability to kill some real meat. I'd had nothing but rabbit and squirrel since I'd feasted on the big cat. But I knew the caliber of the 380 was too small to bring down anything but small game. The shooting of the puma had been dumb luck and really the bones lying at the bottom of the gorge could just as easily been mine as the puma's.

I heard branches breaking and something coming through the woods as if whatever it was was blind. The morning had been coolish and I'd worn my puma pelt to keep the chill off my bones while I sat and watched the forest creatures.

The light which molted the bottom of the forest floor with patterns both complex and simple faded as a cloud raced between the earth and the sun. Then I heard something which I hadn't heard in over 120 days.

"Shit!" a voice called. It wasn't really a shout, but also not a whisper.

My head, complete with puma helmet, shifted in the direction the voice had come from. The sun blotching the monochrome of the forest floor prevented me from seeing who had spoken. Then simultaneously the sun-splotched floor of the forest lit up and the person who had spoken moved.

Fascination! The owner of the voiced obscenity was a young female. She was dressed in cowgirl blue jeans, wore a big bling-bling belt buckle, a flannel shirt with a common pattern, hiking boots, a green vest, and a straw cowboy hat.

"Shit! Shit!" the young girl said as she tried to pull her hiking boots from the tangled skein of vines.

I knew better. I should have simply stayed hidden and let the girl, who was easily my age, fight her way out of the vines. But... but... whether or not I was wanted for stealing horses, whether or not I had essentially murdered that man didn't seem to matter as I stood from my crouching position and moved toward the girl.

I wanted to be her hero! It was as simple as that.

What I'd forgotten was I was wearing the puma pelt. I'd

grown so accustomed to it when I was in the woods. I felt more a part of what was going on in the woods when I wore it. If I'd have only thought about it, what happened next might not have happened.

She told me later she saw me first from afar. She said it looked like the largest puma she'd ever seen. At first she thought she was seeing things. Like some phantasmagoric image which would disappear into smoke if she only blinked her eyes. She did blink several times, but the large cat simply kept moving toward her—directly toward her.

She saw me. I was sure of that. She was, after all, staring directly at me. But the expression on her face seemed to be saying something besides, "Hi there." I hadn't spoken because I'd become so accustomed to not speaking for the past four months. When I got close I would speak. That's what I kept telling myself as I kept on a direct path toward her.

She kept pulling her hiking boots up trying to get herself untangled. The vines pulled themselves tighter and tighter around her double H boots. She confessed to me it looked like she would be an easy target for the big cat. The cat wouldn't have to run after her, he wouldn't have to pounce; all he would have to do was walk! He would walk right up to her, take a bite and start chewing.

I found myself grinning from ear to ear. I hadn't smiled like that since before Dwight had been taken away by his grandparents. In fact, my mouth was wide open in a tooth-filled, full-blown smile.

To her horror, my smile was none other than the big cat bearing its blood-thirsty teeth. I couldn't be any more than twenty feet from her now. She tried to look away, but much to her chagrin, she couldn't. If she was going to get in a cat-wreck, then she supposed she was going to watch the wreck happen.

Then, something else she told me later, there below the big cat's ears down past its open maw she thought she saw a human face—it was a boy—his face was twisted in agony. It must have been the face of a boy the cat had previously eaten. But how could she be seeing such a thing? It had to be something someone who was about to die saw! What else could it be? She felt dizzy, terribly dizzy, and as the big cat closed the gap her eyes rolled up into her head and she fell to the floor of the forest like the first of the autumn leaves.

The sun had gotten lower since I carried the girl into camp. Nearly an hour had passed. She must've been scared to death.

The first indication she was coming around was a low moan from her throat. I'd placed her on the sleeping bag, the saddle as her pillow. I'd also built the fire back up. It wasn't summer anymore and the camp got cold shortly after sundown.

I made coffee, and a steaming mug was in my hands when she first saw me. I still had the puma pelt on and it startled her a little, but not like it had. Out in the open around a nice campfire in the afternoon light she could tell it was a man, or more probably a young man, who sat there sipping on his coffee.

"You want a cup?"

At first she must have thought there was someone else in the camp—someone who was behind her. She couldn't turn and look without giving away the fact she was awake.

"You like coffee?"

Still no answer from the bedroll. I knew she was awake. I'd seen her eyes squinting. Now, they were nearly squeezed shut—nobody slept like that!

"Not answering is answering, you know?" I persisted. The young girl was determined to pretend to be asleep. *Some people*, I thought.

I got up, poured a second cup for her, and set it near the bedroll. I figured the coffee smell would do my talking for me.

In a minute or two, after she'd peeked at me with one eye (I pretended I hadn't seen her looking at me), her arm crept from the bedroll as her slender fingers wrapped around the cup and pulled it toward her. The coffee was still hot and she slurped loudly so as not to burn her mouth.

"Not bad," she said in a much smaller voice that she'd yelled, "Shit!" in when I first saw her.

"You might find a ground or two in it. But that's what happens with cowboy coffee."

She sat up and shucked off the remnants of the bedroll. She took another loud drink. The coffee was still on her upper full lip when she asked abruptly, "Are you going to rape me?"

"I'm pretty sure that's not on my list of things to do today."

"Then, why am I here?"

"You passed out."

"So?"

"So, I couldn't leave you there."

"So, you brought me here?"

"That's right."

"Are you going to kill me?" she asked in a matter of fact manner.

"No."

"My parents are probably crazy with worry over me," she said as she glanced at her expensive watch.

She saw me look at her watch.

"You can have it—the watch—if you let me go."

"You can go anytime you like. I'm not holding you."

She jumped up and threw the remainder of the hot coffee at me. Some of it got on me, but most of it ran harmlessly down the big cat pelt. By the time I'd wiped the drops from my face she was nearly at the beginning of the woods.

"I wouldn't go that way."

"Why not?"

"The sun will be down soon."

She cast a look at the sinking orb.

"The woods will be dark before anything else."

She paused at an opening to those selfsame woods. She was ready to run pell-mell into the woods away from me. I was her danger and I was sure I probably didn't smell or look to inviting. She was like a frightened filly. She might run. She might not.

"I could saddle up the Roan and give you a ride to your parents. Do you know the general direction your camp is in?"

She didn't answer, but nodded twice.

"You stay there. I'll saddle up."

By the time I had the Roan saddled and ready to go she had moved back to the fire and was warming herself.

We took off about the same time as the sundown was fading in the west. We rode the Roan back to where she'd gotten tangled up in the vines. She was able in the fading light to guide me back to a trail she'd taken. She pointed the direction she'd come. Her parents' RV was parked off that trail, but she wasn't sure how far down. She had an argument with her parents and walked off when they were not paying her any attention.

I heard the generator before seeing the lights from the RV. The girl still had her arms around my waist and she was sound asleep. I didn't want to wake her. Those arms felt good around my hard, flat stomach, and besides, I'd never had a girl touch me like that.

By the time the RV came fully into view, I could see several fish and game jeeps parked nearby.

She woke up and slipped from the back of the Roan, then ran for the RV.

I didn't wait for her to get there. The Roan pirouetted where it stood, but before we were out of earshot I could hear raised and relieved voices welcoming the young girl back.

43

had the Roan's left rear hoof captured between my legs. The farrier's apron held it as I pulled the old, worn shoe off.

It amazed me that I'd not forgotten the things I'd learned from certain individuals. The people, I'd eventually forget. But those beneficial things—those I remembered. Maybe I shouldn't forget the people, but over time that's what happened. For example, that man, God rest his soul, had taught me how to trim horses' hooves and also how to shape new shoes and pound them into place. It still amazed me that nails could be driven through horses' hooves without hurting them.

The final shoe was finally on the Roan. The horse had the patience of Job. She'd stood there and pretty much let me do whatever till I was through.

I was through now. I stood up slowly. I supposed this was what it felt like to be old. My back was hollering as I came back to my full 6 feet 1 ½ inches of height. Placing my hands on the small of my back, I twisted to the left and right. A small "pop" happened with each turn—possibly two "pops" when I twisted to the right. That felt better.

I wouldn't have to trim China's or Tia's hooves yet, but it would be tough on them if we got into rocky country. They were barefoot, which served them well in the grassy meadow, but not so much in other places.

I'd known all summer eventually I'd have to move base camp.

Now, the move was imperative. The young girl had seen the camp. She'd seen me. She could probably tell I wasn't that much older than her. There were all sorts of reasons for a young man my age to be spending time in the mountains. Yet, I didn't feel like matching wits with the local game and fish police.

Surely, a BOLO had been put out on me as soon as the folks at Rock Ranch had found the bloated and swollen body of that man covered with flies. It would take the local constables time to put two and two together and come up with my number which would be somewhere between ten and fifteen years as a guest of the state of Montana.

The boys at Rock Ranch made a field trip each year to the old Montana State prison in Deer Lodge. The idea was the boys would make a neat turn around and decide in the face of that ancient prison not to continue their life of crime. Every year the small, punative cells caught our imaginations, but it was the prison cafeteria lunches which eventually turned our stomachs away from wanting to pursue behaviors that would land us at Deer Lodge.

I didn't bother to wipe out traces of my having been there. What would be the point? I didn't care if they knew I'd been there, I simply didn't want to be there when they got there. In fact, not destroying evidence of my having been there would probably keep law enforcement busy enough to slow them down and that was fine by me.

I got the sawbuck saddle back on Tia and let her stand there a bit to get used to it.

"Remember, girl, you wore this on the way up here," I reminded.

I gathered what remained of my possessions—I was shocked how little there was, but then again, the extra holes I had to make in my belt should have told me my caloric intake had been way lower than it should have been for the past few months.

The hunger I'd felt hadn't eaten into my muscle yet. I was

sure of that. Each morning I flexed my biceps and they seemed to be the same size, but maybe that was relative to my smaller body size? Who knew?

I placed everything I had left in the duffel bags I borrowed, well, stolen, from the dead man. Was that really stealing or simply using what was available? I wasn't sure about that one. I used the barrel hitch on both duffel bags securing them to the Xs at the top the sawbuck saddle. Tia accepted all this like it was what she was supposed to be doing.

Truth was, I wanted to get up on the Roan and see if the Cowboy was anywhere around. Even so, I knew the Cowboy was everywhere. I hoped the Cowboy had scored me positively for helping the lost girl and getting her back to her family. I prayed the Cowboy would show me the way to my next place of refuge.

I remembered the thirteenth beatitude, which Dwight had taught me; Blessed is he expects nothing, he shall never be disappointed. I really wasn't expecting anything in particular. I simply knew the Cowboy would find a refuge for me.

Didn't the 121st Psalm say it right out loud:

"I will lift up mine eyes unto the hills, from whence cometh my help,

My help cometh from the Lord, which made heaven and earth.

He will not suffer thy foot to be moved: he who keepeth thee will not slumber.

Behold, he that keepeth Israel shall neither slumber nor sleep.

The Lord is thy keeper: the Lord is thy shade upon thy right hand.

The sun shall not smite thee by day, nor the moon by night.

The Lord shall preserve thee from all evil: he shall preserve thy soul.

The Lord shall preserve thy going out and thy coming in from this time forth, and even for evermore.

As I spoke these last words I was riding away from my summer hideout. Tia was attached to the Roan and China was attached to Tia. We were like the Trinity—three in one.

I really wasn't all that worried about being followed. i should've been, but I wasn't. My experience had taught me law enforcement was inept at best. They might bring their heavy artillery and helicopters, but when push came to shove they usually operated best on a paved surface. If they tried to follow me, I could elude them, this I was sure of.

By midmorning I made it off Teton Peak and was traveling northwest. I didn't want to get out on the plains east of Teton County. I would have stuck out there and been run down like a dog, so I kept to the foothills and whenever possible sought out the cover of the trees. I didn't want to dive right into the forested areas because that would've made traveling more time-consuming. I stayed away from the forested areas and skirted the edges.

And I never bothered to look behind me. I didn't know how important it was to check your back trail. If I would've looked behind me I would've seen a small dust cloud. I found out later that dust cloud was being kicked up by Sheriff Goodman and his deputy riding hell-bent for leather toward my location. I also found out the Sheriff had been taught to read signs by a Blackfoot medicine man, and to Sheriff Goodman I might as well have been marking my trail with phosphorescent paint just asking to be found.

By afternoon of the same day Sheriff Goodman could see more than just my dust cloud. With his powerful binoculars he could make out me, the Roan I was riding and the string of two ponies which trailed behind. That's when the Sheriff made a decision which he later told me he instantly regretted.

Me and my three horses were just across the valley riding along the ridge top.

The crack of the rifle ricocheted across the valley and echoed sounding as if there were other diminished shots fired someplace else.

My head snapped in the direction of the shot fired. Even the shot echoes didn't throw me off. Immediately I saw the two riders on the other side of the gorge. If I sat still right where I was I figured they would catch me in less than twenty to thirty minutes. But the shot hadn't landed anywhere near me. I supposed they had actually fired a warning shot. Thanks for the warning, guys, I thought as I kicked the Roan into a lope.

Tia and China were grazing, but their heads were soon caught up by their halters and the last morsel of grass they had torn off dangled from their mouths like green beards.

I had my triple string of horses over the ridge line and heading down to the swale. Dragging two young horses after me would slow me down enough so the Sheriff would catch up before the late summer sunset.

I turned to the two young fillies following me.

"Don't worry girls; I'm not going to leave you behind. Either we all escape or we all get caught," I said trying to reassure not only the young fillies, but also myself.

I realized I had to get out of the open. I reined the Roan into a wooded area with lots of downed trees. The young fillies, Tia and China, had trouble operating their back legs as they traversed over the deadfall. The going would be slow, but the direction we were taking was counter-intuitive. No one trying to escape would take this particular non-path. Twenty minutes into the maze of trees I could hear the heavy hoof beats of the two horses which later I learned were owned by the Teton County Sheriff's Department. The sound was muted by the buffer of trees we'd passed through. I figured it wouldn't take the Sheriff's deputies long before they would read the lack of sign on the trail. At that point they'd probably double back. By the time they found the spot where I'd entered the tree maze perhaps I would've reached the other side and then we could pick up speed.

My gamble paid off. The copse of trees me and Tia and China had made our way through had lasted less than a mile. Leaving the deadfall and tangle of trees behind I found myself in a meadow which followed a small river north. I kicked the Roan in the sides and within 25 feet all three horses were in a steady gallop, following the river.

By the time Sheriff Goodman read the sign which showed where me and my three horses had passed into the woods, it was too late. In fact, by the time the good Sheriff and his deputy had entered the overgrown forest with all its deadfall, me, on my Roan, followed by Tia and China were making our way out of that same woods.

There are times in a person's life in which, if they could see the future, they might turn around and give themselves up to an alternate future. None of these thoughts, however, even played near the margins of my mind. I simply wanted to make my own way on my own horses—even if they weren't really my own.

What I really missed was the intervention of the Cowboy. I wanted to know if the Cowboy was still with me. Yes, I'd had experience of the Cowboy always being with me, but now I longed for a vision—the vision of a strong and willful Cowboy who would literally take me under his wings and protect and guide me.

I killed a man without really meaning to, I stole horses again — even though they felt like my horses—and once again I was being pursued by the law.

How could I—in the eyes of the world—be on the wrong side of the law and still be on the Cowboy's side? How does that work? I wanted to know.

Then I remembered the story of the shepherd boy David. A story my mother had read to me from the Bible.

A story about a young boy chosen over his older and manlier brothers to be King of Israel. A young boy, David, who had taken the weapon used to protect the grazing sheep onto the battlefield against the Philistines.

He'd taken the slingshot and faced the Philistine giant Goliath. He'd not only faced Goliath, but he had run toward the seventeen foot tall man with nothing but smooth stones and cured leather.

King Saul had given his armor for him to wear in this decisive battle, but David had set the King's armor aside—not because he hadn't prized the gift—more because running in oversized armor would have simply slowed him and the smooth stones down. Later Saul turned against David, as the old have a tendency to turn against youth and agility. Turned against him from the moment he heard his own army cheer for David and pick him up from the feet of the dead giant and carry him on their shoulders through their camp. Saul too, had cheered, but in his stomach he now carried the smooth cold stone which had ended two giants' reigns—Goliath's and possibly his.

Was David on the side of wrong when the Army of Israel and the King of Israel, Saul, had hunted and tried to kill him? No, the Father was still with David even to the point of allowing David to remain King after he sent Uriah to his death in order to access his wife, Bathsheba.

The prophets had said King David had a heart after God's own heart. An adulterer, a murderer, and a seducer—this man had a heart after God's own heart?!

As I rode farther and farther north into the valley between the mountains, I was sure I was on my way to my next teacher—perhaps even a man sent from the Cowboy, Himself! Maybe even the Cowboy, Himself!

It was late summer in Montana. This far north it was almost 10:30 PM before the sun set. I slowed my ride, as I could tell the yearlings were exhausted. After all, they'd spent their entire time on Teton Peak playing and eating. If they ran at all it was for short distances in a game of chase.

Several times I had ridden over toward the stream to give the horses ample opportunity to drink. And drink they did. The third time, the sky to the east was darkening, turning the deep purple of a bruise and following that there was surely the black of a Montana night.

The horses wandered over toward the grassy expansion of the meadow and ate hungrily. I let them eat for a while before I took them down by the river bank where an oxbow had eaten out the side of a giant boulder.

Back under the rock overhang I built the fire, not worrying whether anyone saw the smoke. If the deputies hadn't caught up with me by now, then they'd simply lost my trail. The Cowboy had been with me. I'd escaped once again, escaped north in the land of the north.

As I sat around the campfire I reloaded the Spanish automatic pistol, the Starr Modelo. I counted the rounds I had in the clip. There were only five. I knew better. Being chased like I had been, I should have had a full clip and one in the chamber. I methodically thumbed the small 380 rounds into the clip, slammed it home, and ratcheted a round into the firing chamber. Out of habit I thumbed up the safety. No sense in shooting myself or one of the horses.

Off in the distance I could hear the yipping of the coyotes. I would sleep with the gun across my chest and my hand resting on the butt. Surely, I would hear the yipping coyotes coming before they caused much trouble.

45

Me, my Roan, Tia, and China made it through the night without incident. We had traveled the previous day not stopping till the last light was bleeding from the sky.

When I awakened I was in no hurry. I went down to the creek—which was really the Middle Fork of the Flathead River—and bathed with the only sliver of soap I had left. I was reminded it was Ivory soap as it slipped through my fingers and floated downstream. After a leisurely breakfast consisting of the next to the last can of pinto beans, I saddled up the Roan and gathered what remained of my belongings and placed them in the pack which Tia seemed more than willing to carry once again.

We were running out of everything. Well, *I* was running out of everything. No more soap. No more beans. There was about a cup and a half of corn grits left in the bottom of the bag and that was about it. Of course, the horses had everything they needed—plenty of sweet grass and clear, mountain stream water.

I should have been worried, but I wasn't. I wasn't sure why I wasn't worried, I just wasn't.

"Maybe this is what it feels like when the Cowboy lives inside you," I said out loud.

I was surprised I'd spoken out loud. It certainly wasn't the first time I'd done so, nor would it be the last. But since leaving my four-month camp on Teton Peak I kept my voice and thoughts to myself.

Tia, China, and the Roan stopped eating and turned their heads to look at me.

"Well, maybe it is," I said to the four of us.

This seemed to satisfy all three as they turned their hungry mouths back to the sweet grass. I didn't know why but I felt confident that 1) I would not starve, and 2) I would find a new home soon. And not just find a new home, but a place where I would somehow be a valuable member of a society. That I would be a part of a meaningful group of people, doing meaningful things. I laughed to myself. This didn't cause the horses to look up. They liked my laughter—it was like salt in their sweet grass. I laughed to myself to think a murderer, a horse thief, and an escaped prisoner could be anything valuable to anyone. But it didn't make the feeling of my own self-worth go way.

We followed the Middle Fork of the Flathead River northwest, passing through the Bob Marshall Wilderness. I knew if I kept going north I was going to be in a world of hurt when winter came around, but still within me I carried the Cowboy and I was sure the Cowboy wouldn't steer me wrong.

There are benchmarks in a person's life. Certainly losing one's parents at the age of ten is one such benchmark. Everything which happened to me after my parents' death was affected by that death. Sometimes, these benchmarks make you stronger. Sometimes they tear you down. There's a real sense in which I would not be who I was today without the loss of my parents.

So many events had transpired since my parents' death. So much water, as they say, under the bridge. At this point in my not-so-long life—I was only fifteen years old—I was longing for some direction. Well, naturally, the main direction I was longing for was away from the law. Through a series of misunderstandings and unfortunate timings I had been labeled. A horse thief, a thief, a runaway, an escaped prisoner, a vandal and now, thanks to that man, a murderer.

As I rode into the Bob Marshall Wilderness in north-central Montana I wanted above all things to simply disappear and not in the sense of dying. I could hold the Spanish 380, the Starr Modelo, to my temple and check out, but how much fun would that be? I had always felt killing oneself excluded the possibility of surprise and surprised was one thing I was about to be.

In the morning I ate the only can of beans left. Afterward, squatting in the underbrush, my belly felt like it was about to explode. The beans came rushing out with a horrible sound and even once I'd wiped with the handfuls of grass, my stomach still didn't feel right. What I needed was a good, hot meal with meat, potatoes, butter, gravy and fresh baked bread. Where was I going to find such a meal? It was beyond my imagination.

I rode half that day. The horses were behaving; neither Tia nor China were trying to stop and graze as I pushed to make time. The Roan felt good, and the shoes I'd nailed to its feet while camped upon Teton Peak had stayed solidly on. I checked them that morning when I picked all the horses' hooves. I worried about the yearling fillies. They had never been shod so I picked the routes I took as best I could to protect their feet.

Being rocked back and forth on a horse was so meditative, but suddenly I realized I was being watched.

The first sign came from Tia who simply stopped in her tracks and stared off into the woods.

The Great Bear Wilderness was not called the Great Bear Wilderness for nothing, and this thought occurred to me now. Grizzlies were not uncommon in this wilderness; in fact, it was the persistent and ever present grizzlies which gave the wilderness its name.

I wasn't sure how horses acted around the silver-tipped monsters, but I was fairly sure they didn't simply stand and gawk in their direction. Now China and the mounted Roan were staring off in the identical direction.

What the hell were they hearing, or seeing? I thought, but before I could voice that question the roar of a motorcycle broke the silence.

A bearded man, and I mean he had a really long beard, was

riding a Harley Davidson down a fire road in our direction. I was fairly sure the man wasn't law enforcement and I was also fairly sure he wasn't a Hell's Angel, unless of course he'd been magically transported to the Montana woods from somewhere in California.

Before I had a chance to react to the motorcycle, a Jeep came into view further up the firebreak road. For a moment it looked to me as if the open-top Jeep and the motorcycle were playing chicken. My money was on the Jeep.

Moments before the vehicles collided, both turned in my direction and came screaming after us. Shouts could be heard from other parts of the woods and various motors were being started up.

It was a no-brainer, those pursuing me were obviously aboard motorized vehicles, therefore I would head for the underbrush and as off-trail as I could get and as quickly as we could get there. To my left was the base of a steep hill and the side of the hill was covered in underbrush and overturned logs. I kicked the Roan and encouraged her up the steep slope.

This was in total agreement with all the horses since all they really wanted to do was to get as far away from the screaming engines as they could.

Someone once said, "In riding a horse, we borrow freedom." The ascent up the side of that mountain was the reenactment of that sentiment. I felt like my own legs were striding up the side of that hill. What an amazing feeling.

I glanced behind me just in time to see the Harley flip backwards, throwing its rider to the ground.

The Jeep charged part way up the hill before it crashed into deadfall hidden by the underbrush. The driver was thrown into the steering wheel. He yelled out, grabbing his chest. His passenger wasn't as lucky, as he flew over the front of the Jeep striking his head against the deadfall. The Jeep's engine died and it rolled backwards down the hill.

By this time riding the Roan, with Tia and China following, I made the top of the hill. I didn't look behind me, but kept along the ridge line. One of the men chasing me, the rider of the toppled Harley, pulled a rifle from a scabbard. He raised the rifle, ratcheted a shell into the firing chamber and took careful aim. He was following me on the Roan. Why I didn't come down off that ridgeline, I'll never know.

Right before the shot was fired the butt of a shotgun was rammed into the back of the Harley rider's head. He dropped instantly.

I could see the man wielding the shotgun. He was well over six feet tall. He wore an open drover's coat and a large Stetson hat. His boots were stuffed with striped wool pants which were held up by wide suspenders.

"No one shoots the boy or any of the horses unless they wish to die a very painful death!" the voice boomed past the large salt-and-pepper beard all the way up to the ridgeline. If the truth be told he looked a whole lot like pictures from my history book of the abolitionist, John Brown.

"The boy and horses must be caught without harm to them!" His voice carried up the side of the mountain, but did not reach the other Jeep as it came to a stop.

The driver of that Jeep raised a rifle and was aiming at me when I saw the side of his face explode.

Down below, John Brown ratcheted the 30/30 expending the spent shell. "I'm not kidding about this, gentlemen!" he bellowed.

"Cowboy?" The word escaped my mouth without me even being conscious of my mind forming that word.

I pulled back on the Roan's reins.

"Whoa!" I said as my eyes met John Brown's eyes.

"No harm will come to you, son, I promise. All I want is to make you an offer," the man's words reached the crest of the hill with no trouble at all.

I stayed mounted and followed the motley group of men back to their camp. I expected to see tents and camp fires. Not so. What I saw absolutely astonished me. It was like a picture out of a history book. The men who had surrounded me and hundreds of others had built a fort—like the forts I'd seen in cowboy and Indian movies. A guard tower marked each of the four corners of the fort and the men standing guard brandished Browning automatic rifles.

A shooting range had been built on the outside of the fort walls. Large berms of earth had been piled up and men with rifles and handguns fired off rounds at paper targets. The *pop pop popping* of the handguns and the cracking of the rifles broke the silence of the forest, but to me the sound brought comfort.

I wasn't stupid. This group of men and their leader—obviously the man in the drover's coat was their leader—they weren't exactly within the boundaries of the law. For one, this was a national forest, and building in one was against the law unless you were the government. Besides, hadn't the leader killed one of his own men with impunity? He had to be the leader. Displaying the power to kill at random showed absolute leadership with absolute power.

This had to be one of those survivalist groups I'd read about who lived, it seemed, all over Montana.

How surprised I was when we rode through the main gate. Children were playing and running about; women were hanging up clothes and chatting with one another.

Rooms were situated all around the stockade. Each room had one wall which was in common with the outside wall of the fort. I tied the Roan to a pole that supported the walkway along the inside of the fort. I was shown to an inner room and told to wait.

The room was decorated in a rustic, Western-style. The couch was big, black, and leather and was covered by a large Navajo Chief's blanket. The colors in the blanket were red and gray. A four directions cross was woven in the middle of the blanket surrounded by varying shades of gray.

A large wooden desk the size of a six-person dining room table sat stoutly in one corner of the room. A gigantic chair covered with brown and white cowhide slumbered behind the desk. Proudly displayed in the middle of the front of the desk was a Frederic Remington sculpture of a cowboy lassoing a calf.

I took a seat in one of the straight-backed shaker chairs in front of the desk. On the edge of the desk, a painted plate was propped up on a stand. This, too, was a Remington. A singular cowboy riding a grey horse gripped his reins in his left hand and a rifle rested in the crook of that arm. With his right hand he held a pistol skyward. He was hatless and had a long, white moustache. The engraving on the plate read: *The Flight*. I supposed it was named that because there were eight Indians in hot pursuit behind him on the plains.

I'd barely made myself comfortable when the door to the office opened and the man who looked like John Brown walked in. He dramatically swirled off his drover's coat and hung it on the hall tree inside the door.

I half expected the man to look reduced once he'd taken off his hat and coat, but the effect was entirely opposite. Instead, he looked enhanced. It might have had to do with the pair of pearl handled 44 Magnum single action pistols which hung from the Mexican leather gunslinger's belt. Or maybe it was the hide vest which sported the short hairs of a brown and white young calf long dead.

He sat in the chair behind the desk. It groaned under his weight, not because he was a huge man, but more because the chair was old and the wooden pegs strained to hold the antique swivel chair together.

"That was kind of interesting the chase you gave us," he began.

"Is that what it was?"

He laughed out loud. His laugh was sharp and caustic. I could almost feel the laughter tear at my flesh.

"Good! Good! I like that. You're an honest young man."

"Actually, I'm wanted by the law."

"Hold your head up, son, being wanted by the law is not always a bad thing."

"Isn't it?"

"You know it isn't! Tell me, what have you done that makes the law interested in you?"

"Where do you want me to start?" It was an honest question and I wanted to simply tell my story to another living being. So tell my story I did.

I started with my parents' death and didn't leave one thing out. The big man sat back in his chair and listened. At times he laughed. Once I thought I saw a tear in his eye. For quite a while he leaned back with his eyes closed. If it hadn't been for his hands, which were crossed on his chest and continued to move, I would have thought the man asleep.

The man's hands listened as well as the man's ears did. His hands opened in surprise when something puzzling happened in my story. His hands curled into fists when I was taken to Rock Ranch.

His fingers formed a temple when Dwight and I became friends and balled into fists when the man whose name I shall never mention again turned a budding friendship into an opportunity to take advantage of a young man's sexuality.

When I described my escape from that man's ranch, Arthur Bannack (I learned later that was his name) opened his eyes and sat forward in his chair.

The rest of my journey, from my escape from Rock Ranch to now was spoken right into the open eyes of the man who was definitely listening. When I finished, the leader of this survivalist group stood up and paced back and forth in front of his desk. Finally, he turned to me.

"The Cowboy you talk about in your story, do you still believe in him?"

"Absolutely!"

"That's good. That's good. I want to tell you something which you may not understand, but which you must believe!"

I didn't speak.

"May I tell you my dream?"

"Yes."

"My dream was about this place, this refuge which I and others like me have carved out of this wilderness. In the dream, men who do not want me to be here, men who are opposed to my way of life came here with guns and armored vehicles to take away what we have made here. We tried to escape but they had blocked all the roads with their police vans and their half-tracks. When we tried to fight back, they overpowered us with their firepower. We thought we were done for. Many of my friends, their wives, and their children lay dead around us. There seemed to be no escape. We vowed to fight to the last man, but all we really wanted to do was escape.

"We thought all was lost, when we heard a thundering. We looked to the sky thinking it was about to rain or maybe they were sending military jets to destroy us.

"I looked in the direction of the thundering, which was growing louder, and then, I saw you.

"You were riding a Roan like the one you rode today, but instead of two fillies behind you, he had a string of horses—fifteen

153

or sixteen of them. They were all saddled up.

"You rode into the fray as if you didn't fear death. Twigs shot from falling branches as you rode along, but not a single hair on your head was touched and the horses were also unharmed. You rode to where we were hunkered down. We all mounted up and were able to escape.

"And it was all such a surprise. We were all laughing, riding and laughing. Tears of joy filled my eyes as I rode up alongside you. You turned to me and said, 'The cowboy sent me.' And the tanks, halftracks and military vehicles could not follow just as you showed us today."

The man stopped speaking and he stared at me.

"Did the Cowboy send you?"

"The cowboy has been with me since my folks died five years ago. Wherever I go is somewhere the cowboy has sent me."

"What's your name, son?"

"John Wilson Barnes."

The big man extended his handsome hand and I took it in mine.

"Arthur Bannack. It's a pleasure, my boy, a real pleasure."

I mmediately after Arthur and I talked, Arthur called a meeting of all members of their camp. Women, men, workers, children, cooks, carpenters—everyone stood on the parade grounds of the fort and waited for Arthur Bannack to appear. Conversations among those present stopped the minute Arthur and I walked out of his office.

Arthur stood before the multitude and literally looked out on every one of them. If possible the crowd grew even quieter. Finally Arthur spoke.

"God, the Father Almighty, has sent us all a special messenger today. If you'll remember your Greek and Hebrew you'll remember the word for messenger in both languages is also the word for Angel.

"This Angel," he said as he grabbed my shoulder and pulled me close, "this Angel has brought us nothing but good news. My condolences go out to the friends and family of Mike Baldwin. I shot and killed Mike because Mike was about to kill our angelic messenger."

I felt weird for several reasons. First, being the cause of another man's death, but then again, I'd already been the cause of the man whose name I'll never mention's death. I'd learned to live with that. I was sure I could and would live with the idea that this Mike Baldwin, if he had not been shot, would have certainly been the cause of my own death. The second thing which was weirding me out was what he'd said about God, the Father Almighty. I hadn't said God had sent me here. It was the Cowboy who had been with me since my parents' death. It was the Cowboy who had sent me here. Then as Bannack spoke it came to me. *Perhaps the Cowboy and God, the Father, Almighty, were one and the same? Could that be? Was God a cowboy?*

Arthur continued, "Starting today, motorized vehicles will be phased out. Their use here at the fort and all our other enterprises will eventually come to an end. This country—this rogue country, this United Shits of America—is dependent on foreign oil and the whims of the big petroleum industries. We here at the fort will no longer be beholding to sand niggers or corporate hosers.

"John Wilson Barnes, this young man right here, will be responsible for training horses and the people who will eventually ride horses. If we want to survive in the future, we must go back to the past.

"A long time ago we made a pact with the horse. He was our ride into town. He pulled our groceries and goods back from town to our places of residence. He brought the doctor in the buggy when we reproduced ourselves. He followed us into war and gladly died by our sides. He carried our bodies to the holes in the ground where we wait for the eternal and everlasting resurrection. He was our companion in times of trouble and our peaceful rides in the long shadows of our afternoons.

"We will again renew our eternal and everlasting contract with the horse and by this stepping back we will be eons ahead of those who have tied their wagons to science and modern technologies. We no longer wish to be a part of scientific discoveries any more than a fly wishes to befriend a can of Raid.

"In the book written by John of Patmos we read these words,

"And I saw heaven opened, and behold a white horse; and he that sat upon him was called faithful and true, and in righteousness he doth judge and make war. His eyes were as a flame of fire, and on his head were many crowns; and he had a name written, that no man knew, but he himself.

"And he was clothed with a vesture dipped in blood: and his

name is called the Word of God. And the armies which were in heaven followed him upon white horses, clothed in fine linen, white and clean.

"And out of his mouth goeth a sharp sword, that with it he should smite the nations: and he shall rule them with a rod of iron: and he treadeth the winepress of the fierceness and wrath of Almighty God.

"And he hath on his vesture and on his thigh a name written, KING OF KINGS, AND LORD OF LORDS. And I saw an angel standing in the sun; and he cried with a loud voice, saying to all the fowls that fly in the midst of heaven, Come and gather yourselves together unto the supper of the great God. This was from Revelation 19:11-17.

"If, in fact, it was good enough for Jesus and his followers in the biblical apocalypse, it is and will be good enough for us here at Fort Apocalypse."

Cheers rose from the crowd as those in front pushed forward to shake my hand. Some of the women hugged me and the young girls kissed me. The men said they were proud to know me. I had just scored a major coup and all I had done was ride into their camp. In one moment I'd gone from being wanted by the law to wanted by the people.

It had been settled. I was now a major part of Fort Apocalypse and best of all again, I was training horses for people and people for horses.

The next few months for me were both confusing and exhilarating. In some ways I felt, for the first time since my parents' death, there was a man who wanted to be my earthly father. I felt Arthur Bannack both loved me and expected a great deal from me. It was exhilarating, but also I knew there was a price to pay.

Being loved was easy and the expectations put upon me by Arthur were expectations I both desired and wanted to fulfill.

48

Over the next few weeks, the majority of the men were busy cutting down trees and building a barn and sleeping quarters for their new wrangler. Once again I was to be sleeping with the animals I loved best.

The barn was way too big for me, Tia, and China, but Arthur Bannack explained that soon the huge barn would be filled with the finest horseflesh Montana had to offer.

This wouldn't be as expensive or difficult as one might imagine. People had trouble feeding their horses in winter. Hay was expensive and scarce.

One day, while the building continued Arthur picked me up in his F-250 Ford.

"Where we going?"

"To buy the horses you're going to train."

We had to use the four wheel drive on the Ford until we ran across Federal Route 2, which ran across northern Montana from Bainville in the East to Troy in far western Montana.

The first place we stopped was at a ranch which had a large horse trailer for sale.

Arthur didn't haggle over the price and counted out one thousand dollars in one hundred dollar bills. The trailer was older, but had a nice place for tack in the front.

"You could have talked that rancher down, you know?"

"You mean I could have used less of these worthless pieces of paper than I did?" Arthur asked, taking a wad of bills from his vest and spreading them on the console between us.

"Yeah, maybe as much as five hundred less."

"Do you have any idea what's behind this cash? These greenbacks?"

"I don't understand."

"I like it when a man knows his limitations. You're right. You don't understand."

Author took a handful of hundred dollar bills and threw them out his window. The bills flew up and scattered behind the trailer.

I gasped involuntarily. He'd probably thrown out more money than my own father had made in a year.

"You see," Arthur said, "most people are so invested in this printed money that they think it has intrinsic value."

"It doesn't?"

"Absolutely no value at all. You can exchange these bills for goods, but you cannot exchange them for actual wealth. They print 'silver and gold certificate' on the bills, but if you drive to Fort Knox and try to exchange them for real gold or silver? Well, you just see how far you get."

"But people work their entire lives for money. Sometimes they die for it."

"It's a crime, that's what it is. A crime to think these green bills are worth anything. Real wealth is land, clothes, buildings, your health, and also your horses."

Arthur's bargaining, which essentially was no bargaining at all, continued with the horses he purchased. Whatever price the rancher quoted him Arthur smiled, nodded his head and pulled out his wad of cash.

When the trailer was full with eight new horses, Arthur drove the F-250 back to the spot where he would have to four-wheel it back to Fort Apocalypse.

I took a saddle from the back of the Ford and saddled up what I thought was the most rideable of all the horses. The rest of the horses had the leads to their halters tied to the tail of the horse in front of them.

The lead to the first horse was tied to the D ring on my saddle and I led them back to the fort.

Most of what happened next I've pieced together from stories told me, or from accounts I read in newspapers and such.

Arthur drove out on Federal Route 2 again and this time he headed west. The first town he came to, he parked in front of the local bank, put his drover's coat on and snatched a coach side-by-side from under the back seat. He reached through the split beside the right-hand pocket of the drover's coat and held the 12 gauge side-by-side along his leg. Nobody remembers seeing a man carrying a shotgun down the street and into the bank so he must have hidden it in some manner.

As he walked toward the bank's front door, he pulled the white polka dotted wild rag up over the lower part of his face. Inside the bank the only person there besides the bank workers was an older fellow, who was the bank guard. The woman who survived said the bank guard smiled at Arthur. Under his wild rag Arthur might have smiled back, I wouldn't have put that past him, then drove the butt of the side-by-side into the old man's forehead. The guard's knees buckled and for a moment he looked like he was praying, then he fell forward onto his severely wounded face.

Sitting behind his desk out in the open, the bank manager reached for something. He stopped cold when Arthur lowered the side-by-side and blew the closest bank teller off his stool with both barrels.

Cordite and smoke filled the bank as Arthur calmly broke the side-by-side open, flicked out the expended shells with his fingernails and reloaded, snapping the gun closed again.

"What'd ya do that for?" the bank manager demanded. He was in his fifties with a full head of white hair.

"I assumed you were the only one who could open the vault otherwise you'd be sprawled out on the floor."

"You damned fool—it's already opened!" The bank manager came back without really thinking.

Arthur now saw the vault door was standing wide open.

"So it is," he said as he swiveled the 12 gauge and blew the top of the manager's head off and up against the wall.

The full head of white hair now looked like a large guinea pig walking down the wall.

The only remaining employee, a young, not unattractive woman at the second teller's window screamed. She was the one who supplied all these details. She said she'll be lucky if she can ever forget anything about that awful day.

Arthur pulled the side-by-side in her direction and she stopped screaming.

"Ma'am if I have to kill you, then I'll be the only one who could load the cash into these garbage bags," he said as he pulled two black garbage bags from the pocket of his drover's coat and tossed them in her direction.

"Fill those bags full and you live," was all he had to say to send the female teller snatching up the garbage bags and scurrying into the vault.

"Make it quick. I'm sure someone has heard the shots and is calling the Sheriff's Department. If the Sheriff gets here before I leave with the full garbage bags you will die with me in a hail of gunfire."

From the vault could be heard the plastic sounds of the bags as they were being filled. The female teller ran out of the vault, pulling the full garbage bags behind her.

Arthur stopped her with his free hand and peeked into the vault.

"Good work and fast!"

He took a better look at the thirtyish female teller. Her hair was disheveled and she had sweat pouring off her face and staining her underarms.

"You wouldn't want to join us, would you?" Arthur asked

totally serious.

She shook her head emphatically.

With that he shoved her back into the vault and began to close the door.

She ran toward him shouting.

"I'll suffocate in there. The manager is the only one who has the combination."

Arthur stopped her by placing his hand against her ample chest.

"The invitation's still open," he said cocking his head to one side.

She backed away from his hand into the vault muttering as she did so.

"I'll simply run out of air," she whined.

Arthur raised the shotgun.

"I can take you out quick, if that's what you want."

The teller began to scream.

Author slammed the heavy vault door closed and spun the lock, then the tumbler.

The bank guard must have regained consciousness and reached for his gun. It was still in his hand when they found his headless body.

49

The town of Cut Bank, Montana was small. It wasn't one of those shrinking towns which had once been mediocre sized and the tanking economy and flight to the cities had shrunk it. It started out small and stayed that way. It was on the edge of the Blackfeet Reservation and Indians, as well as whites, stopped in at stores, drank the liquor they bought in its liquor stores, and yes, they all at one time or another, had used the Cut Bank National Bank. After my time with the Fort was done, I'd gone to Cut Bank and stood outside the bank trying to imagine what it must have looked like on that fateful day.

The bank was open that day, but not for business. The street leading up to the bank and the street along the side were crammed with every sort of police car around. Most were Ford Galaxy 500 Police Interceptors, the vehicle of choice for a great deal of police departments. All that was different about the Galaxy 500s was how they were painted. They ran the gauntlet from flashy Glacier County Sheriff's cars and Blackfoot Tribal Police cars to the more sedate, but armed to the teeth, FBI and ATF vehicles.

Ambulances and more vehicles also lined the middle of Main Street waiting for the medical examiner—an overworked man in his late fifties who hadn't seen this much carnage since his second time in Korea as a Corpsman—to make announcements as to the causes of death, even though every corpse was obviously gunned down.

The medical examiner had been ready for the past hour to

make his pronouncements, but had—as a courtesy—waited for the FBI and ATF to get there.

Meanwhile, one of the bank employees, a young woman in her mid-thirties, was unaccounted for. Telephone calls had been made to her house phone and her cell. No one was at her home. She was a single mom and her only child was in the fourth grade at the local elementary school. Finally, someone noticed her purse in the break room. This confirmed she'd been at work and was now obviously missing.

Mary Sills may have been taken as a hostage, or simply run away during the robbery, however the fact that she was possibly in the airtight vault which was closed and locked couldn't be ignored.

Calls had been made to other banks in the effort to find out the combination, but that search had been futile.

Welders were called off from local jobs and their acetylene torches had been spitting at the vault's hinges and locks for forty-five minutes with no result besides the acrid smoke produced in volumes.

The last law enforcement officer to arrive was Lawrence Miller, Senior ATF agent in all of Montana. He parked his car on the side street and walked the block and a half to the bank.

Lawrence Miller was fifty years old and a Negro, even though he hated that nomenclature. He was six-foot-three, trim and one hundred ninety-five pounds and his daily workout regime would have inspired Jack LaLanne, even though the majority of his ATF Associates didn't know who Mr. LaLanne was.

Lawrence was known all over Montana as he was the chief alcohol, tobacco, and firearms agent in the state. He'd had many opportunities to advance, but his love of horses and his three hundred acre ranch outside Darby, Montana in the Bitterroot Valley kept him in Montana and according to agent Miller, it also kept him sane.

Agent Miller made his way past the gathering crowd and

relatives of those who had died inside and walked up the three short steps and through the open doors of the bank. After getting to know Miller the way I later did, I can easily see his assured gait as he made those three stairs and entered the bank. The man was a grand entrance without trying to be one.

"Nice of you to make it before rigor mortis set in," came a comment from the senior FBI agent on the scene. Agent Miller pointed at that agent.

"You, I forgot your name—"

"Sam Tilley," came the reply from the agent, who obviously was miffed Miller didn't remember it.

"You've told me your name before and I don't remember it. What makes you think I'm gonna remember now?"

The FBI agent simply shrugged his shoulders.

"Do something useful and shut the bank doors."

The FBI agent seemed confused.

"I'm talking to you, No-Name. Go shut the doors!"

The agent from the FBI went over to shut the doors, but he grumbled the whole way.

"I've been briefed on what's happening here," Miller said.

Miller turned to the welders.

"Stop with the torches!"

"Hey!" said the insulted FBI agent, "there's probably a lady teller in there."

"Well, have you searched the body of the bank president?"

"No combination on him, sir," said one of the newer ATF agents.

"Did anyone search his desk?"

"Nothing there, sir," said the same newbie.

"Uh huh," was all Agent Miller said as he walked over to the desk.

Miller pulled the top middle drawer out and turned it over dumping the contents on the top of the desk.

"We already went through that stuff," said the insulted FBI

agent who was still standing by the closed bank doors.

Miller simply pointed to the bottom of the desk where a slip of paper was taped.

"Somebody try these numbers on that lock," Miller suggested.

The newbie grabbed the slip of paper, ran to the vault, and began spinning the tumbler. On the second try, the vault's lock clicked and he was able to open the door.

Miller stepped into the vault and put two fingers on the carotid artery of Mary Sills' neck.

"Someone tell the paramedics to come in here and work on this live one," Miller said as he backed out of the vault.

The other law enforcement officers, FBI, and all the other ATF agents parted like the Red Sea before Moses as Miller walked into the center of the bank.

"Tell the coroner to please bag these bodies!" he ordered. The newbie ran out to tell the coroner. "Have all the pictures been taken, evidence numbered and collected?"

All the officers shook their heads yes!

"Then let's have a pow-wow as soon as the bodies are removed. I think I have an idea who's behind this carnage."

The bank lobby was cleared of the bodies. Relatives outside wailed and moaned; well, the women did. The men's eyes welled with tears and they wanted to hit something. So much for the sexes being the same.

Lawrence Miller sat at the desk of the president of the bank. Behind him, an exclamation mark was drawn in blood where the top of the bank president's head had slipped down the wall. Miller had chosen his seat carefully—if their eyes weren't on him, then they'd have to be on that bloody smear. He expected a lot of eye contact and he got it.

Mary Sills had been revived and it was determined there was no brain damage from a lack of oxygen. Nevertheless, she was taken to one of the doctor's offices in town for this to be confirmed.

Agent Miller sat still, without speaking until the miscellaneous chatter completely died down. The film and projector were brought from the back and set up.

"Were going to take a look at this recorded robbery, but I can tell you from the way the bodies were shot up this is the work of the same man which has terrorized banks and savings and loans across the state of Montana."

The grainy film was in black and white. It revealed the man in the drover's coat, his entry into the bank and the killings in their order. There was no sound, but the violence of the images caused many seasoned officers to either look away or flinch.

Miller stopped the projector as the man in the drover's coat placed his hand on Mary Sills' chest and prevented her from exiting the vault.

"Gentlemen," agent Miller began, "What we have here is the first and so far, the only time, this desperado—"

There was some laughter at Miller's use of that word.

"You all saw what this man did to each and every employee of the bank up until this point. If you think 'desperado' is to strange a word for him, then I suggest you think again. This man has absolutely no regard for human life, yet here he is negotiating with the young lady. Why? What did he say to her?"

Miller stood at this point and came around and sat on the edge of the desk.

"This is the first and only break we've gotten in these cases. This man," Miller pointed to the screen, "this man kills wantonly and has to this point never, ever left a witness. Mary Sills is the key to us cracking this case. After she is further examined by doctors she will be interviewed and she and her child will be put in protective custody."

"You have any idea who this guy is?" asked the newbie, the only one brave enough—or stupid enough—to interrupt agent Miller.

"That's a good question and I'm glad you asked it."

The newbie glowed as the rest of the agents glowered at him.

"I do have an educated guess but until I've talked to Ms. Sills I'm going to keep my guesses to myself. When we make guesses what we do is limit how we see things."

When Agent Lawrence Miller got to the doctor's address, the doctor was all but through with his examination. Miller was waiting for him when he exited the tiny private room.

"How is she, doc?"

"Are you a relative?"

Miller flashed his ATF badge. "I'm the agent in charge of this investigation."

"Sorry, you can't be too careful these days. The patient, Mary Sills, is in fine shape. I must say if she had to stay in that vault much longer she wouldn't have made it, though."

"Can I talk to her?"

"Certainly. She'll be out in a minute."

Years later Miller told me what impressed him about Mary Sills was how vibrant and alive she was when she exited the exam room. Immediately it caused him to think of those who had been gunned down.

"Mary Sills?"

"Yes?"

Agent Miller showed his badge.

"I'm Agent Miller with the ATF. Alcohol, tobacco, and firearms. I'd like a word with you, if I may?"

"The Sheriff's deputy told me he'd take me to my son after this."

"I can take you there. It's of the utmost importance that we talk."

"Can't it wait?" Mary asked, as Miller helped her on with her coat.

"I'm afraid not. What happened today at the bank has happened a dozen times across the state. As far as we know, you're the only living witness this man has left."

"He touched my breasts!"

"I know, I've seen the film."

"I thought he was going to gun me down in that vault!"

"He must have liked you."

"He *touched* me."

"Can you remember what he said to you?"

"I want to see my son, now!"

It was warm in Agent Miller's car. The late fall day had taken a turn for the worse and Miller's feet were beginning to thaw in the blast of his car's heater.

"Here's something you'll need," Miller said as he reached into the back seat and handed Mary Sills her purse.

"You turned the wrong way," she instructed.

"Your boy is at your house, not at school."

"He's there alone?" she shrieked.

"No, a deputy is with him."

"He doesn't care much for men."

"It's a female deputy."

"That was thoughtful."

"Are you going to remember what the bank robber said to you or will we need to call in a hypnotherapist?"

"Bank robber, my ass, excuse me, he's nothing but a murdering bastard!"

"If it's any consolation I think your assessment is correct."

"It isn't!"

"Fair enough." There was a pause in the conversation. "So, about remembering—"

"I know exactly what he said to me. Every word. I won't need any encouragement."

"Are you sure?"

"He said—and I quote, 'You wouldn't want to join us, would you?'"

"He said, 'us' did he?"

"He said, 'You wouldn't want to join us, would you?'"

"When did he say this?"

"Right after he touched my chest."

"Is that all he said?"

"No. When I told him I'd suffocate in the vault, he said—and I quote, 'The invitation's still open.'"

"Was that the last thing he said?"

"No. When I backed away into the vault shaking my head, and I said I'd run out of air in there, he smiled and said—and I quote, 'I can take you out quick like if that's what you want?'"

"So, basically he offered to shotgun you to death?"

"Yeah, what a gentleman, huh?"

Mariah's face was twisted, and she looked like she was about to cry.

"Hey, it's important you remember, I didn't know any of this until much, much later. As far as I was concerned Arthur Bannack was simply an eccentric survivalist who had lots of money."

"Didn't you stop and think about where he might have gotten the money?"

"Darlin', I was fifteen years old. I didn't know whether to scratch my watch or wind my ass. What did I know?"

"Grandpa, you lived with this man!?"

"Yeah, honey, I did, and I was also there when he died."

ary Sills got out of Agent Miller's car and ran to her front door. The door swung open while she was halfway up the steps, but there was no one in the doorway. Miller stopped backing out, pulled his weapon, cocked it and aimed through his car window at the front door of Mary's house.

Mary's nine-year-old son stepped into the door frame with the female deputy right behind him. Miller pulled his aim away and uncocked the piece. There came a call across his radio.

"Oh boy," he said to himself as he answered the call.

The garbled talk from the static-filled radio was unable to be ciphered except by the most seasoned veterans of such calls. Miller listened for a long while, rolling his eyes at one point.

"Yes, sir, I know, sir."

Again there was a lengthy part of the call while Miller listened to the static.

"You really want my recommendation?" he keyed in.

There was another static-filled answer which was way too long for a simple yes or no to which Miller keyed this response.

"The witness, a Miss Mary Sills, will be put in protective custody along with her nine-year-old son. Since she is the only living witness, she should be placed far away from the state of Montana. I believe the bank robber is a part of a larger group probably one of those survivalist groups. If he's spending all the money he's taken, which I think he is, this is one hell of a survivalist group."

I worked with the horses Mr. Bannack and I had bought. I still wasn't sure why Mr. Bannack was so loose with his money. Why he wouldn't barter with the ranchers? The ranchers purposely raised the prices on their horses so when the bartering began they could still get a decent price. I'd watched the faces of the ranchers when Mr. Bannack had simply agreed and pulled out the wad of cash. They wanted the man's money, but they wanted to work just a little harder to get it. To my way of thinking, not bartering and paying top dollar Mr. Bannack was actually making himself unpopular with the ranchers.

As I worked with the horses I tried to keep my mind and heart with the feel of the horses. I maintained eye contact with the various horses as they went through the drills, but my heart just wasn't in it. I was too worried about Mr. Bannack and the large group of folks I'd inadvertently become part of.

This was obviously an illegal settlement. They had built their fort in the Big Bear Wilderness. I knew this because all the wilderness areas in Montana, or United States for that matter, were protected from squatters. But here they were some five hundred men, women, and children living on federal land without the permission of the federal government.

But why were they here? And why would they accept Arthur Bannack's total control over them? It worried me how Arthur Bannack could simply take out Mr. Baldwin (who obviously was going to shoot me), and not worry about any repercussions?

There was only one person I'd ever heard about who would

act in such a way and get away with it. I'd read about this man in world history class at Rock Ranch. The man's name was Adolph Hitler.

Late summer turned into fall. The aspens, maples, and elms shouted out their colors into the sunny, but cold, skies. Finally, as fall came to a close, north winds blew what remained of the colorful foliage into the interior of the fort and onto the floor of the newly constructed barn.

So much had changed so often in my life I actually had the Fort Apocalypse carpenters recreate the barn from Rock Ranch, right down to the tack room where Dwight and I had spent so many happy years together.

I had them build bunk beds, and I slept on the top bunk. It was warmer up there and besides, if I couldn't see the bottom bunk I could pretend Dwight was down there listening. Each night I poured out my heart to Dwight like I'd once poured out my heart to the Cowboy. Every once in a while I climbed aboard Tia and talked to the Cowboy, but I hadn't seen him in such a long time. It worried me. Was he around and not showing himself? I couldn't figure it out.

Talking things over with Dwight was more comfortable, not because I was uncomfortable on Tia or with the Cowboy, but because the top bunk was warm and more times than not I simply fell asleep as I opened my heart to my old friend.

Hey, I was glad Dwight wasn't there. Glad because one of the principles which governed Fort Apocalypse was the hatred of all people of color. When they were being nice, the people who occupied the fort called them (the people of color) the mud people.

Mud people were stupid, didn't have the high intelligence of white people, and were forever trying to mate with white men and women. The mud people knew they were inferior and hoped to improve their lot in life by intermarrying with whites. This, of course, according to Arthur Bannack, never worked. Inter-

175

marriage always created more mud people and nothing else.

I didn't understand this kind of thinking, and I didn't believe it anyway. Dwight was actually smarter than me and I knew it! I couldn't, and wouldn't, hate Dwight simply because he was more tanned than I was. Actually, smiling to myself, I would say right out loud, "Dwight was more colorful than I was."

One evening my daydreaming was interrupted by a knock at the tack room door.

"Come in," I said as I jumped down off the top bunk.

Arthur Bannack entered and stood beside the door. Whatever else this man was, he showed a sense of his place and that was, of course, my place.

"Please have a seat," I said as I gestured to one of two chairs around a small table.

Arthur sat down and simply stared at me. I gazed back at Arthur. This was the way lots of our communicating began.

"You know what I like about you, John Barnes?"

"I feel there is a lot to like about me, sir, but there's no telling with other people what they do and don't like about you."

"You're right. You're right."

There was an uncomfortable moment of silence between me, the fifteen-year-old boy, and the grown man.

"How are the horses doing?"

"Well sir, I work with them on the ground a lot before I even put a saddle on one."

"And, I hear you don't really break them," Arthur added one eyebrow arching skyward.

"If you break something you just have to fix it. The way I learned—from a lot of experience and a lot of mistakes—is to allow the horse to do some thinking on his own. They're flight animals, you know?"

"No, I didn't know that."

"Yes, sir, they want to run away when they're scared,

confused, or not used to something."

"Like a lot of people I've known."

"Is that right?"

"Yeah, lots of folks want to talk the talk, but not many want to walk the walk."

"I wouldn't know about that, sir."

"No," Bannack said shaking his head in agreement, "you really wouldn't, would you?"

There was another uncomfortable silence between us.

"And how about the riding lessons?"

"I'm surprised how many of these folks have actually ridden before. With them it's a bit harder than teaching the ones who've never ridden—"

"Why's that?"

"The way I teach riding—the gentle way which stresses understanding the horse before you ride him—the way I teach riding, it's harder to break the ones who think they know how to ride. I mean, it's harder to break them of their old horse habits than it is to teach someone who barely knows anything about horses."

"Then it should be harder to teach me. I've been on a horse since I was four years old."

"Actually, sir that may be a plus for you. How would you rate your riding skills?"

"Well, I haven't been on a horse in years, so, it's hard to say."

"We can begin tomorrow, if you like?"

"Tomorrow I'm going on another buying trip. How many horses do we have now?"

"About thirty head, sir, quite a nice remuda, if I do say so myself."

"Then, we need about twenty more and we'll be set."

"But sir, there are nearly five hundred souls here at Fort Apocalypse."

"True... true. Have you ever been on an ocean liner?"

"I haven't even seen the ocean."

Bannack barked a laugh, rubbed his face with his hands, then rocked back in his chair.

"Most ocean liners don't carry enough lifeboats for all the passengers, did you know that?"

"No, I wasn't aware of that."

"There is a reason they don't. When catastrophe strikes at sea and lifeboats have to be deployed, the nature of the situation is usually such that only those passengers and crewmembers above the waterline will ever have a chance at survival. So, why crowd the decks with lifeboats which will never be used?"

There was a pause while Arthur Bannack inspected his hands.

"I'm not sure I'm following you, sir."

"You know the name of this Fort?"

"Fort Apocalypse, sir."

"And do you know what *apocalypse* means?"

"No sir, although I think it has something to do with the Bible."

"Uh-huh, sort of. It means the end of time as we've known it. You see it doesn't mean the end of time itself, but only the end of time as we know it. When an apocalypse happens there's a shift in time. If you're ready for the shift, you continue to enjoy having a relationship with time. You continue to live. If you're not ready for the shift of time, then your time comes to an end. You understand?"

"What does this have to do with lifeboats and horses, sir?"

"The horses are our lifeboats in a sea of uncertainty and chaos. The reason I've only sent you a certain number of people to learn how to ride is these will be the only people who have a chance when catastrophe strikes."

"I like it here, sir. I don't want our time here to end!"

"Neither do I, but it will end. Sooner, I'm afraid, then later."

"And those who don't have horses?"

"That's the beauty of my plan. They love it here like you do and the love of this place—which I consciously chose—the love of this place will incline them to protect it and the way of life we have created here. But, alas, it can't be protected or preserved. There is only one immutable law in the universe and it's change. All things change."

"This place will change?"

"Oh yes, in the blink of an eye. It will turn from the paradise we have created into a battlefield rife with the blood of those without lifeboats—"

"Without horses?"

"Exactly and their fighting spirit and love of what we have created here will buy us, those with horses, the time to escape."

I wasn't sure how I felt about all the people left without a way out. Arthur rose from his seat and placed a hand on my shoulder. He often did this as a way of saying the discussion is over.

"Do you understand?"

"Yeah, I mean, yes sir, I do understand," I said still not sure why so many would be left behind and so small a group escape.

At the door Arthur turned.

"I won't be needing you to go with me this time."

"Are you sure, Mr. Bannack?"

"Positive, and I believe you're right."

"Right, sir?"

"I will barter with the ranchers. It's what they expect, so why should I disappoint them?"

I stood up. It felt strange to be seated when the big boss was standing.

"The reason I want you here today is to teach my mom and dad to ride."

"Your mom and dad are here?"

"Yes. Mother's name is Bertha and dad's Ed."

"Shouldn't I be more formal with them?"

Arthur walked back to the table where I was standing beside my chair. He put a hand on my shoulder again.

"They don't make 'em like they used to anymore, do they, John?"

"We are all unique in the Cowboy's eyes."

"That's so true. It's just some of us are more unique than others. My parents have been herding sheep for the past forty years. They're simple people. They won't care if you call them Bertha and Ed."

"If you say so, Mr. Bannack."

54

ertha and Ed were standing in the arena. Each had a lead rope in their hands. Each lead rope was attached to a horse.

"Why do I need to ride a horse?"

"Just do what Arthur says to do," Bertha shot back at Ed.

"Mind your own business. I wasn't talking to you. I was talking to the boy. Well, boy, why do I need to ride a horse when the only thing I want to do is have a drink—"

Ed shot a look at Bertha and raised the index finger on his right hand.

"Not a word, not a god damn word!"

"If you're thirsty, Mr. Ed, there's a cooler full of water just inside the stables."

"Now, the god damn kid thinks I'm a horse from a 1950s sitcom!"

"I don't understand?"

"Of course you don't. How old are you?"

"I'll be sixteen in two months."

"You can always tell who the young are. They are actually gloating about how young they'll be on their next birthday."

I realized all this talk was getting us nowhere. I decided to change tactics.

"Lead your horses in a circle with you on the inside."

"Which direction?" Bertha asked.

"Either way. We'll do both ways by the time we're finished."

Ed handed the lead rope to John and walked out of the

181

arena.

"Mr. Ed?"

"Like I said, kid. I need a drink."

"But the stables are this way," I said as I pointed the stables out.

"Uh-huh," Ed said, walking back to the main part of the fort.

"Don't worry about it. We used to ride forty years ago and it's like riding a bicycle, right? Once he gets on, he'll remember."

"Whatever you say, Miss Bertha."

"Just call me Bertha."

Bertha was riding around the round corral while I stood in the middle, watching her.

"The horse is trying to tell you something, Miss Bertha."

"Tell him to speak up!" Bertha answered jokingly as she was jostled atop the horse.

"It's a mare, Miss Bertha, a girl, like yourself. And she isn't using her mouth to communicate. She's using her entire body. Look, there, her ears are turned toward you. She's listening."

"What should I say?"

"Pat her on the neck and tell her she's a good girl."

Bertha leaned forward and banged the horse on the neck.

"Pat. Pat. You're not punishing her, you're rewarding her."

"For what? I can barely stay in the saddle!"

"Sit, totally sit, in the saddle. Let the horse feel your weight."

"I'm sorry, horsie; I've been meaning to go on a diet."

I shook my head in bewilderment.

"That's all we'll work on for today," I said, not wanting to tax Arthur's parents too much.

Bertha continued to ride the circle of the round corral.

"Bring her to a stop, Miss Bertha."

"Whoa!" Bertha said as she pulled on the reins. I walked over with a step stool and she dismounted the horse.

"I didn't do very good, did I?" Bertha asked, standing beside the horse.

"You did fine, Miss Bertha. Try to encourage your husband to stay the next time he comes for a lesson."

"Ed won't listen to me. He never has. He thinks women, like children, should be seen, but not heard."

"Well, if we have to use these horses he won't do well unless he's practiced some. So will you ask him?"

"You're a sweet boy, John. How did you get mixed up with these folks?"

"Lucky, I guess."

Bertha came up close to me and spoke in a whisper.

"Luck has nothing to do with anything associated with my son. Don't trust him, boy, no matter what he tells you. He'll turn on you like a cobra in a corner."

Several people were waiting at the round corral gate.

I looked nervously toward those folks.

"I wouldn't be saying things like that about Mr. Bannack."

"He may be Mr. Bannack to you, but to me he's just little Artie," Bertha said, and she walked out of the round corral.

All this time me and Miss Bertha were out in the round pen, Edward Bannack was sitting in a recliner in his room at the fort. A nearly empty fifth of bourbon sat on the floor beside his chair. In his right hand he held a single action Ruger 44 caliber Magnum.

He opened the loading gate on the Magnum and placed one shell in the cylinder. He spun the cylinder and flipped the loading gate closed which stopped the cylinder from spinning. He cocked the Magnum and pointed the barrel beneath his chin and toward the ceiling. At that precise moment the door to their cabin opened. Bertha stood in the doorway.

"Come in, come in," Ed said in a voice which was slightly slurred from the alcohol. "You're just in time to see me win, again."

Bertha shut the door and walked over to the sink where she poured herself a glass of water.

"I can't believe you're still playing that stupid game!"

"It's not stupid, and it takes a real man to play it. Are you ready?"

"I think I'll go watch the others have their riding lessons," she said as she made her way to the door.

"Sit down!" Ed yelled and Bertha physically jumped, then ran over and sat at the small table where they took their refreshment.

"You ready?"

"Ed, please."

Ed pulled the trigger on the Magnum and a loud click resounded throughout the cabin.

"I win again! Hot dog!" Ed said.

He opened the loading gate and violently spun the cylinder, snapping it shut and cocking the piece. He reached down and picked up the bottle and drank nearly all of it, leaving only a corner.

"You ready to see me win again," he said as he placed the barrel under his chin.

Bertha looked out the small window which was situated over the table. Far in the distance the mountains looked serene and beautiful.

"Look at me!" Ed screamed as he stamped his booted feet upon the floor.

She looked just this time see Edward Bannack blow the top of his forehead to the ceiling above him.

55

The scream that came from the cabin which Arthur Bannack's parents occupied could only be described as unearthly and surreal.

I'd almost made it to the doorway when Bertha flung it open.

Bertha supported her husband, Ed, whose entire upper body was soaked in blood.

I recoiled—I'd never seen so much blood, not even when Tia had kicked and killed the man whose name I will never mention.

Finally, I got a hold of my fear and ran up to support Ed. He was literally hanging between Bertha and I.

"The truck, the truck, the truck, the truck..." Bertha kept repeating over and over as if it was some sort of mantra.

We steered Ed toward an older Ford F-100. The keys were dangling from the ignition.

"You drive, you drive, you drive, you drive..." Bertha said over and over again having adopted a new mantra.

"I don't have a license. I don't know how," was all I could come back with.

I got Ed into the cab and scooted in beside him.

"I drive... I drive ... I drive ..." Bertha chanted as she ran around and got behind the wheel.

Bertha started the truck, slammed the automatic transmission into reverse and planted her foot on the accelerator as if she was killing a black widow spider. The F-100 fishtailed out of the spot it was parked in and almost hit someone who was walking behind it.

Bertha then slammed the gearshift into drive and blasted across the compound at Fort Apocalypse aimed toward the main gate. Fortunately, the gate was open because Bertha's foot stayed planted on the accelerator pedal. I wondered to myself if, in fact, she knew where the brake pedal was.

Ed continued to bleed profusely from his massive head wound. At one point I realized my jeans were slipping on the seat because there was so much blood.

The dirt road—if you could call it that—was more tire ruts than a road. Every once in a while the pickup would jump from the ruts as if it were trying to escape its mission which led me to ask, "Where are we going, Bertha?"

Bertha simply stared at me and said one word.

"Hospital."

Once again the pickup jumped from the rutted tracks and ran over small pines which banged in protest against the hood of the truck before they were snapped off and drug beneath the speeding vehicle. This jump from the ruts almost ended us up off the mountain and down into a very steep ravine.

"Do you know how to drive?" I yelled above the sound of the drumming pines.

"I'm learning," Bertha said.

"How long have you been driving?"

Bertha looked at her watch.

"Ten minutes," Bertha replied, her knuckles white on the steering wheel.

I reached under myself into the pool of blood and found the seatbelt. I belted myself in.

By the time we reached the small town of Glacier Park East on Highway 2, Ed was passed out and slumped against me. Both of us were covered in a lot of blood.

Bertha's driving had improved, but the position of her foot had not changed—it was completely mashed down on the accelerator. By the time we reached the hospital at the junction of

Federal Route 2 and State Route 49 there were two police cars with their lights and sirens on close behind us.

Bertha slammed on the brakes and jumped out. I opened the passenger's door and pulled the bloodied Ed from the middle of the bench seat. Hospital staff with a gurney and a wheelchair came running up.

The police were momentarily distracted by the pickup—which Bertha hadn't put into park—as it careened off the emergency circle and idled its way across the hospital lawn.

Hospital workers laid Ed out on the gurney and other workers had shoved me into the wheelchair, above my protests that nothing was wrong with me, but they whisked me toward one of the triage rooms.

Ed, still alive and no one knowing exactly why, was taken directly into surgery.

"I'm OK," I protested as they lifted me from the wheelchair to a gurney. A nurse was cutting off my shirt, my legs were tied down and an oxygen mask was placed over my face.

A young female doctor began to run her fingers through my hair as she searched frantically for the head wound which had caused so much bleeding. An orderly rolled me on my side as nurses sponged the blood off my torso. They were all looking for possible GSWs.

Finally, the doctor took the oxygen mask off my face.

"There's nothing wrong with you," she said a bit annoyed.

I sat up and swung my legs over the side of the gurney.

"Yeah," I said nonchalantly, "I've been trying to tell you all that! The blood is Mr. Ed's blood."

"Is that the gentleman who came in with you in the pickup?" The voice came from the corner of the triage room and it belonged to a Montana State Highway Patrolman.

I immediately grabbed my head, moaned and fell back on the gurney. My feet began to clatter against the gurney. They pulled me back straight upon the gurney and placed the oxygen over my face again.

The Highway Patrolman sauntered over and stood beside the gurney.

"Is he faking this?"

The orderlies were holding me down as my entire body shook. I rolled my eyes back into my head.

"I think he's in shock," the female doctor said.

"But a moment ago he was fully—"

"Shock sneaks up on a person," she said to the patrolman. "Give him a mild sedative ASAP," she directed toward a nurse.

The nurse handed the syringe to the doctor and it was shot into my buttocks. In a few moments, I stopped shaking and lay relaxed on the gurney.

"Can he talk to me now?" the officer asked.

Before the doctor could answer a scream came from down the hall.

"Why don't you talk to the woman who came in with the GSW victim, she seems to be in fine voice," the doctor suggested.

I knew who was screaming down the hall. It had to be Bertha. She was anything but calm. No one would listen to her because she simply wouldn't stop ranting and raving. When she wasn't forcibly trying to enter the surgical unit she was pacing up and down in the waiting room. Her mouth was going ninety to nothing.

The Montana Highway Patrolman left my triage room and walked toward the waiting room. I was feeling pretty good from the sedative, and they'd left me alone momentarily in the room. I got up from the table, grabbed a smock and followed the sergeant. As he entered the waiting room he was immediately approached by a male nurse.

"You're here because of our call?" the nurse asked.

"What call?"

"This woman! We're on the verge of sedating her."

The Montana Highway Patrol Sergeant looked at Bertha. She

was talking fast, real fast and he could make out part of what she was saying and it interested him.

"I'll take care of this," the sergeant said.

"Ma'am," the sergeant said as he tapped Bertha on the shoulder.

Bertha hadn't noticed the tap and she kept on raving.

"Do you have a tape recorder?" the sergeant asked the nurse. "Ma'am, I'm Sergeant Blum with Montana Highway Patrol. Won't you sit down and tell me everything from the beginning?"

Sergeant Blum sat beside Bertha, the tape recorder at his feet. For the first time since Ed blew off the front of his head Bertha smiled.

"Finally, someone wants to listen," Bertha said, as she sat down and more calmly than before started her story from the riding lesson.

56

Helena is the capital of Montana. One might be puzzled how it became the capital. There's a history to that. Be that as it may, it is a smallish town surrounded on the west and south by foothills. The headquarters of the Alcohol, Tobacco and Firearms division of law enforcement for the state of Montana were in an unassuming building very close to the capital building.

Agent Lawrence Miller sat in his smallish office on the second floor. This morning he'd received a telegram from the Montana Highway Patrol. One of their sergeants had been smart enough to record the ramblings of an elderly white woman by the name of Bertha Bannack.

The woman had delivered someone she claimed to be her husband, one Edward Lee Bannack, to a small hospital in East Glacier Park just outside the national Park.

In Sergeant Blum's report he stated that Mr. Edward Lee Bannack had received a self-inflicted gunshot wound to the head. Mr. Bannack was still in a coma after surgery and was not expected to live.

Sergeant Blum's report stated Bertha Bannack had insisted her husband had not tried to commit suicide. In fact, Bertha had said her husband often played Russian roulette with himself once he'd become intoxicated and not once—except this time of course —had Mr. Bannack brought any harm to himself.

Lawrence Miller backed away from his computer and considered that either Mr. Edward Lee Bannack had had an incredible stretch of luck over the past twenty-five years or his wife, Bertha, was a compulsive liar.

The wife was supposed to be detained by the local sheriff's department, but shortly before the transfer (from MHP to Glacier County Sheriff's Department) was to be made Bertha Lynn Bannack had disappeared. One of the receptionists at the main hospital entrance remembered a young man—probably in his teens—hustling Mrs. Bannack from the hospital into a late model Ford pickup. The two of them had sped off together.

Of course, that was me, and how I ever got her out of there without being stopped, I'll never know.

It was decided by ATF Montana a twenty-four hour watch would be put on Edward Lee Bannack. The doctors didn't expect him to regain consciousness and if a relative had been around they probably would have advised taking him off life support.

ATF Montana made calls to ensure Edward Lee Bannack would not be taken off life support. The usual cop outside the door of the elder Bannack's room was not used because ATF wanted to catch whoever came to retrieve Edward Lee Bannack.

The agents who were in charge of this particular stakeout were put directly under Senior Agent Lawrence Miller's control. If anything, anything at all out of the ordinary happened, Agent Miller was to be notified.

Miller was so confident something would develop from this lead he checked into a nice motel in East Glacier Park and even participated in the stakeout.

Miller's participation was mainly limited to showing up at the stakeout site at just about any time imaginable. It angered the Junior Agents who thought they were stuck on a senseless stakeout, but it also encouraged them to be wide awake and ultimately, completely alert. Miller knew they were annoyed, but figured their complete participation in the stakeout was his goal so their feelings about him were inconsequential.

Three weeks into the stakeout, ATF Montana was fairly convinced this particular lead was, in fact, leading nowhere. There was only one reason the stakeout continued and that was Agent Miller's belief something big was connected to the comatose body of Edward Lee Bannack.

Monday was the beginning of the fourth week of the stakeout. The Junior Agents were getting sloppy and even Miller's unexpected visits weren't enough to keep them on their toes. The black Ford F-250 came through the rain mixed with snow as if it were floating on air. Blocks before the small hospital Arthur Bannack had turned off his lights.

The F-250 parked at the side of the hospital and no one got out.

"We'll wait here until the Hour of the Wolf," Bannack said looking straight ahead through the windshield.

I sat in the seat across from Bannack. I wasn't sure when the Hour of the Wolf was, but I was sure I'd know when Bannack left the truck. After a while my head rocked back and I drifted off to sleep. It seemed as if I'd only been asleep for short while, but when I opened my eyes Bannack was not in the truck.

Shit, I thought to myself, *I've screwed up and let Mr. Bannack down—*

Before I'd finished this thought Arthur opened the driver's door and slid in, the interior lights did not come on because they had been removed.

"Did you have to take a leak?"

"I did pee, but that's not why I got out," Bannack replied seriously.

Before I could inquire why Arthur had left the truck there was an explosion that rocked both of us. Flames shot fifty feet into the air and several cars in the main parking lot of the hospital burned like giant wicks on a candle.

Before long gas tanks joined into play and several more explosions rocked the Ford.

"Come on, boy, the wolves are on the move," Bannack said as he slipped from the truck.

The stakeout car was not far from the parking lot, and before the first flames had reached their entire height, the Junior Agent on stakeout had placed two calls—the first to Agent Miller and the second to the fire department.

By the time Miller arrived the fire trucks were trying to keep the burning cars from starting other cars from catching on fire. Another explosion shook Miller's car.

When Miller stood beside the stakeout car, he rapped hard on the driver's window.

The window whirled down.

"What are you doing?"

"Watching the fireworks," came the candid reply from this smiling Junior Agent.

"Have you been in to check on Edward Bannack?"

The smile disappeared from the Junior Agent's face.

The two agents, Senior and Junior, ran past the exploding, burning cars toward the entrance to the hospital.

Edward Lee Bannack's room was empty. The diversionary explosions had brought everyone to the windows facing the parking lot. Agent Miller figured whoever had taken Mr. Bannack from his room had hustled him out the back door and disappeared before the second car had exploded.

The hallways had security cameras in them, and each exit was covered by cameras also.

The Junior Agent couldn't stop apologizing, so agent Miller sent him back to the car to retrieve his camera and take pictures of the crowd was watching the fireworks in the main parking lot. Sometimes... Sometimes those who caused havoc liked to stick around and watch it.

Agent Miller knew whoever had done this was way down the road even before the fire department showed up, but he simply wanted the Junior Agent out of his sight before he said something inappropriate to him.

Miller went down to security, showed his badge, and confiscated the film from the hallway in the intensive care unit and from all exits in the building.

Miller drove past the fires which had barely subsided. The lights from the emergency vehicles and the fire reflected off the safety glass of his car windows. Off to the east, as if in response or perhaps even an echo, the sun was splashing its own red, orange and pinks into the Montana morning sky.

Miller parked his car in front of his room, took the room key from his breast pocket of his dress shirt, opened the door and went in. Just before he closed the door he scanned the woods across the street. One could never be too careful.

He placed the film from the ICU hallway in the projector he always carried in his Galaxy. After threading it through carefully, he turned it on and sat warily on the foot of the bed.

He played it back and forth until he found the happenings following the first explosion. He watched with interest as the figures in the hallway walked like an old-time movie in and out of the various rooms.

Then Miller sat up. His posture became very erect and he leaned forward. He stopped the tape and played it forward. There he was—the man in the drover's coat and black cowboy hat. He was being followed by a teenage boy who had a jean jacket over his pearl snap cowboy shirt. Mr. Drover Coat purposely didn't look in the direction of the cameras, but the teenage boy looked directly at the camera. All he didn't do for correct identification was take off his straw cowboy hat.

A few seconds later Mr. Drover Coat and the boy were on either side of Edward Lee Bannack as he was literally being dragged down the hallway—his feet splayed out and his shoes making black scuff marks on the linoleum floors.

Miller replayed the film several times then picked up the phone and dialed a number he knew well. After what seemed like a long time the phone was answered.

"Chief, this is Miller."

Before Miller could explain, he got an earful.

"I understand, sir, but I've got what I believe to be a positive ID on the serial bank robber/murderer—"

Once again a lengthy pause.

"Yes, sir, I'll be in Helena with the film in three hours, sir, that's why I called—thought you'd want to be there."

57

iller didn't like to talk about his exploits. He was really a modest man. It took years for me to get this entire story out of him.

The main squad room was filled with senior ATF agents and their protégés. The hubbub was louder probably than it should have been, but the anticipation was high. Word-of-mouth had spread Miller's words to the chief that he was in possession of a positive ID on the spree of bank robberies/murders which had plagued the state of Montana for the past two years. It had gotten to the point it was as bad as what the FBI and G-man faced in Chicago in the 1930s. Someone, or some organization, was terrorizing the banking industry in the state of Montana and ATF was taking the fall.

The chief stood up at the podium and by the count of three all the noise was off; all eyes on the chief.

"It's not often we get a break like this. I don't want us to blow it. Thanks to one Sergeant Blum with the Montana Highway Patrol, we got a lead on some suspects whom—after listening to the ramblings of one of their group —we think, seriously think, were involved and have been involved in all seventeen of the bank robberies which have plagued this state. All this comes about because I'm your chief—"

There was general laughter in the room. The chief smiled and even more laughter broke out.

The chief put up his hand and the laughter died down.

"You men, all you agents from the most experienced to the

least, know cases get broken because of the fateful and persevering work of our field agents and there are not many better than Special Agent Lawrence Miller."

The chief extended his hand. Miller stood up and shook it and then took the podium. "This was captured at the small hospital at East Glacier Park."

He showed the film from the hospital hallway. A man in a cowboy hat and drover's coat came quietly down the hall followed by a young man also in a cowboy hat, but wearing a jean jacket.

There was an audible gasp when the man in the drover's coat appeared.

Miller stopped the projector.

"Obviously, this is either the same man from the bank robbery, or it is someone who looks an awfully lot like him. When he comes out of the room he's going into, please notice he's favoring his left leg just as he was when he carried the garbage bags full of money from the bank." The film continued and the man in the drover's coat and the young boy carried/dragged a man from his room. He walked with the same limp while supporting the man.

Lights were turned back up and the film stopped.

Miller was once again at the podium.

"The wife, we believe, of the man taken that night in East Glacier Park from his hospital bed—in a coma I might add—is the same woman whose rambling testimony to Sergeant Blum sort of spells things out for us. Somewhere in north-central Montana a survivalist and perhaps white supremacist group known as Fort Apocalypse is operating. We believe there may be hundreds of them and thanks to the nearly twelve million dollars taken from seventeen different banks, they are probably heavily armed and extremely well organized. Gentleman, I can't stress this enough; this isn't going to be your usual arrest. This is going to be a search and destroy mission on the scale of a major military battle. We're about to go to war, gentlemen, and as in any war, it is kill or be killed."

The sun came up and there were flakes from a gray sky. The snow started out slowly, but by the time me and Arthur had reached the cutoff for Apocalypse the snow was flying sideways from the north. A low-pressure area sat squarely over the south-central portion of Montana and circulation from that low pulled the winds like taffy from the north.

Edward Lee Bannack was propped up between Arthur and myself. He was slumped to the side, and I thought he was dead. I studied the old man whose head was still swathed in bandages.

"He don't look so good."

Arthur didn't even bother to look at his father.

"He'll either live or he'll die, it's up to God the Father Almighty," Bannack said flatly.

I wasn't sure what else to say, so I stared ahead at the great flakes of snow as they danced quickly then shot over the cab of the F-250.

"The snow's a blessing, I can tell you that," Bannock said matter-of-factly.

"It'll make it harder to get back."

"Yeah, but also impossible for anyone to track us," said Bannack.

"Unless it stops."

"Are you kidding me? The way it's coming down and blowing? I heard a weather report this morning which said that a low-pressure is moving so slowly it might as well be staking a claim. We'll be lucky if it stops day after tomorrow."

Edward Lee Bannack suddenly rose up like Lazarus coming out of the tomb. He reached his arms around our shoulders and said, "God, it's good to be alive!"

The Ford F-250 swerved right, then left. If one had been standing on the shoulder of the road as we careened by, one would have seen the men in the front seat with eyes as wide as saucers and mouths open. The sound which came from the truck wasn't really a scream so much as it was two men yelling at the top of their lungs.

The F-250 hit a snow bank on the right hand side of the road and stuck there. Inside the truck, Arthur and I were plastered against our respective doors staring at Ed Bannack who was smiling beatifically.

"It's good to be alive, ain't it boys?" Ed repeated.

"Dad, how are you feeling?" Arthur asked as he unstuck himself from his door.

"Son, I feel great. Like a giant weight has been lifted off me," Ed said.

"You know who I am?" Bannack queried.

"Of course I do, son. Don't have a clue who the good-looking young man is sitting next to you though," Ed said.

I extended my hand across the seat.

"I'm John Barnes."

"Edward Lee Bannack pleased to meet you!"

Bertha Lynn Bannack was preparing for her husband, Edward Lee Bannack's, funeral. Arthur had told her that he and I were driving into East Glacier Park and would be returning with Ed. It didn't look good. Ed had shot himself in the head playing Russian roulette and when people do that, generally they die. But Edward Lee Bannack was a tough, old bird.

Bertha Lynn had put up with his emotional, and sometimes physical, abuse for the past forty years and really, at this point, maybe it was time to have his funeral and put that part of their life behind her.

When she heard her son's F-250 drive in at sunup she prepared herself to see the mortal remains of the man she'd married so long ago.

What she had not prepared herself for was the jovial, and yes, almost sweet man who stepped from the Ford pickup. The man looked like Ed, but Ed never, ever ran to her, picked her up and spun her around.

"Bertha ... Bertha ... Bertha," he yelled as he spun her in three circles and then set her down gently. The activity nearly collapsed him.

Bertha looked at Ed. It was Ed's face that the man wore, but the Ed she had known for the past forty-five years? Well, he was nowhere to be seen.

Still in Ed's arms, Bertha spoke.

"Is that you, Ed?"

"And have I told you lately I love you?" Ed responded. From the way she looked at this man, she obviously didn't think it was Ed. Maybe she thought it was someone who looked like him with a bandage on his head.

"You do know I love you, don't you, dear?"

She told me later she never remembered him calling her 'dear' not even when he was courting her.

"Is everything all right?" Ed inquired.

The slap Bertha gave Ed could be heard all the way across the compound. As Ed's head snapped sideways it occurred to me perhaps a hard slap in the face was not the best thing to give a man who'd blown part of his brains out.

"Are you mad at me, sweetheart?" Ed asked.

It was then Bertha started screaming.

"What have you done with my husband? Where have you taken him? I expected a funeral, not a resurrection!"

Arthur grabbed hold of his mother and walked her to his quarters. Bertha was babbling as he marched her off.

Before he interceded, he asked me to take Ed to the stables. Ed's face burst into a giant smile.

"I love horses, I absolutely adore them!" Ed said as we walked toward the stables.

Arthur took his mother to her quarters while Ed and I messed with the horses. Before I knew what was happening, Ed jumped on one of the saddled horses and took off to the large outdoor arena.

The horse and the man moved as one. Honestly, I'd never seen a man ride a horse with such feel and understanding. In a few minutes, Arthur and his mother ventured out to the arena.

"That's the way he rode when we first met," Arthur's mother said mystically.

"He rode like that?" Arthur matched her tone. "He should have been a cowboy, not a sheepherder."

"Sheep were cheaper than cattle. Plus they kept renewing their crop of wool and reproducing the numbers that were lost."

"He should have been a cowboy," Arthur said once again as he and his mother watched in awe.

Ed took a spill off the horse, landing on his back in the arena. The horse turned around to check on Ed. Evidently, the horse had enjoyed having him on his back.

Ed was lying down with Bertha seated beside him. Arthur and I stood by the door, not sure what to do or say.

Arthur moved closer to me and whispered, "Why did you let my father get on that horse?"

I guess I looked surprised. "I didn't *let* him do anything. He saw the saddled horse, jumped up on it and took off into the arena. He's a masterful rider," I added with the great deal of respect.

"It's the way he used to ride way back when. At least that's what mother says."

"When he gets better, can he work with me?"

201

Arthur looked at me and placed his hand on my shoulder. I knew he was getting ready to leave.

"You bet. We'll need more than just you to gather the horses when 'they' show up."

I looked at Arthur with concern. "Who are 'they'?"

"We'll know when 'they' show up. You can stay if you like, but I've got work to do."

Bertha sat with her face in her hands. She wasn't crying. She was too angry to cry. Ed reached out and touched Bertha's knee. Bertha jumped like she'd just placed her wet finger in a 220 socket.

"I'm sorry, hon," Ed whispered.

Bertha reached out and took her husband's hand.

"Ed, in the past forty years you've always been one mean son of a bitch," Bertha said softly.

"I know, Sug. How do you think I feel about that?"

"I never really thought about how you felt about anything. I simply tried to avoid you when you were angry."

"I've killed my anger."

"What does that mean?"

"I'm done with pushing you around. I'm done with guns. I'm done with the booze. I think I'd like to live on the other side of life now."

"But we've never lived on that side."

"We could give it a try."

"I'm too old to change."

"I've changed," Ed said as he took Bertha's hand again in his.

"Yeah," she replied, "but you also blew out your brains."

Ed smiled. "Whatever it takes, Sug."

59

We didn't know it at the time, but all Montana ATF agents, senior and junior, were involved in some way, shape and form in the search for the survivalist—and perhaps white supremacist—group known now as the Apocalypse Group. No organization, it was understood, would call itself apocalypse unless somewhere down the road they expected an all-out conflagration. All agents were warned to proceed with caution since in seventeen robberies there was only one survivor.

Agents filled helicopters, and agents straddled four wheelers and ATVs. But one agent in particular had his own personal mode of transportation. Of course that was Agent Miller, the man who would enter my life like all those who entered did. It wasn't like I was looking for him, but when he appeared, I knew he was the next one in line. Funny how life presents people to you? If you're not prepared you may not know they're gonna be the next major person in your life, but if you just let things happen around you, you'd be surprised at what comes up. How was I to know at the time that this colored man searching for a white supremacist group was actually searching for *me*? Of course, the same thing could be said of Agent Lawrence Miller, he had no idea either. I guess that's why over the remaining years of his life he told me how it all came about.

The Dodge D-Series pickup truck made its way past East Glacier Park and proceeded on into the wilderness. It pulled a horse trailer. Off the paved road it followed a forestry trail up and up as it wound through the Rocky Mountains in the Big Bear

Wilderness. When the last Forestry Road gave out, the truck pulled to a stop. It was in the middle of the road, but that didn't matter much when the middle of the road was also the end of the road.

Agent Miller didn't bother locking the truck. This far into the mountains it wouldn't matter. If someone wanted to break into the truck or steal it they would. Agent Miller packed the single action Ruger 44 magnum pistol. It only held six shots and it had to be cocked by hand before it would discharge a round, but that's why Agent Miller liked the piece. It wouldn't go off unless you really meant it to. He carried the .44 in an old army holster with the leather flap closed over the butt of the gun and secured by a metal protrusion which was larger at its very end. The leather strap had a hole in it which pushed down over the shaft of metal.

Agent Miller knew his weapon was from the nineteenth century, but it didn't matter. Yet, when a hollow point .44 caliber hit home the damage was extensive and deadly. Be it a three hundred pound man or a nine hundred pound grizzly the bullet would maim, if not kill, its intended target. Not to be outgunned in an emergency, Miller also carried in a shoulder holster beneath his vest an Army-issue 45 automatic.

There was only one horse in Miller's trailer and it was already saddled. The Colorado Saddlery saddle was heavier than most, but it was also sturdier. Miller liked the way his frame rested in that saddle and so did the seventeen hands high black horse named Beauty.

Beauty's black mane and coat glistened in the meager sunlight which was able to find its way through this primal forest. Miller knew people would think the horse's name was perhaps feminine—although, the horse was a gelding—but he also knew and believed the horse's color and stature said something about him.

If black was beautiful, then Agent Miller astride black beauty was quite a sight to see. Miller liked to think of them as black beauty squared.

Miller urged Beauty up the nearest rise toward the top of the closest ridge. He wanted perspective on where he was. He carried no maps and relied on his instincts when searching. He knew if he became disoriented he could give Beauty his head and the horse would unerringly take him back to the trailer and the truck.

The day was hot and dry. The breeze was high up in the Ponderosa Pines and whistling nicely, but not stirring at the base of the trees.

Miller had been riding for five hours. He'd seen lots of things; mule deer, elk, a snake which slithered away as he approached, and some lost cattle that probably wouldn't make it through winter. And yet he hadn't seen hide nor hair of anything which looked like a survivalist camp. In a way, he was glad but in another way he felt guilty. Guilty like he'd taken the day off to go riding when there were killers out there. One killer in particular. He didn't like even the idea of a man like that being among other human beings. He did, however, like the idea of that particular man spending the rest of his life in jail. And secretly, as many agents did, he wished he could catch that particular man in the act of a felony and using the judge strapped to his side take the man out for good.

Black Beauty was breathing audibly and Miller realized he'd have to get off the ridges where he'd hope to catch some sign of the settlement and go down a swale into the valley and catch up with a pond or stream.

Miller descended easily on Beaute—that's what he liked to call the horse—and fairly soon he heard the trickling sound of a stream. He got to a point where he could actually see the stream, easily two hundred yards below him as it slipped over rocks. The dissent directly to the water would have been foolhardy so he zig-zagged the side of the mountain.

Eventually, the sound of the stream was so loud it was all he could hear. Up ahead a short drop joined the smaller stream to a larger stream. Around the bend of the hill he could see an area which had pooled out, a perfect place to water Beaute.

As he and Beaute made the short drop, slipped through the muddy bottom land (the horse nearly sat back on his haunches at one point), then rounded the corner, he saw something which surprised him greatly. A saddle horse with its nose deep in the pool. Off to one side, a slender cowboy had his hat off and was also drinking from the same pool.

The running water had kept both the horse and the offed rider from hearing their approach. The horse noticed first, flinched and whinnied loudly. The slender cowboy looked up, his hair wet and water running down his neck.

Miller couldn't believe his luck. The slender cowboy was none other than me, the boy who had assisted the drover coated man who snuck Ed Bannack from the clinic/hospital in East Glacier Park.

"Howdy."

Miller touched the brim of his hat. "How do?"

"I'm doing better now that I've found this pond," I replied.

Miller's horse, Beaute, found his way to the pond and started drinking. Miller stayed saddled up. He had two choices. The first choice he eliminated right off the bat. He wasn't going to arrest the slender cowboy, whom now he could tell was an adolescent. No, he had his .44 magnum and the boy was unarmed. Arresting the boy would have been foolhardy. First, the boy might not talk and torturing adolescences was not part of the ATF's way. Secondly, he ached to find out more from this boy, say his goodbyes, then double back and follow the lad. All this flashed through Miller's mind in an instant as he dismounted and scooped water up and washed his face with it.

"You lost, son?" Miller asked. Immediately, he regretted the question.

"No more lost than you, sir," was my candid reply. I smiled as

I said this and the smile was genuine and from my heart. Miller didn't know why, but immediately he liked me. You can just tell sometimes when somebody likes you.

Miller laughed out loud and I joined him in his laughter.

"I don't mean this to sound racist but you're the first colored man I seen in a while."

"No offense taken, son," Miller said. I especially liked the way the word son sounded.

"I used to have a buddy, Dwight was his name. He was colored. I taught him to ride, and in the end he was a damned good horseman."

"Most people think coloreds look funny on horses," Miller said. I wasn't sure why he was being so straightforward.

"Then, most people don't know their U.S. history, do they, mister. I mean, what about the Buffalo Soldiers?"

"You got a point there, son. I like the way you think," Miller said meaning what he said. He was probably wondering, right then and there, how this boy, who obviously had a colored friend, could be associated with a white supremacist group?

"You and Dwight still hit the trail together?"

"No, sir. He got reunited with his white grandparents in Boulder, Colorado. We wrote for a while, but I haven't heard from him in what seems ages," I said, not sure why I was talking so much—maybe it was because the man reminded me of Dwight.

We let the conversation lag. We looked at each other across the pond. Up high the wind still whistled in the pines. The horses got easy with each other and drank deeply. Finally, I broke the silence.

"Where you headed, mister?"

"No place in particular. I have a job which has a lot of stress and sometimes—not as often as I'd like really—I try to just get away from it all. You want to ride a ways together?" Miller asked.

"Sure," I said, "why not?"

I knew Miller was no fool, and I also knew that he knew

whatever direction I took would be exactly the opposite direction from the group of people I belonged to. It was only natural for me to keep the group safe. So I did what he expected me to do, I took Miller away from the group.

"Do you believe in the Father?" I asked.

"You mean," Miller began, "the man upstairs?"

I laughed. It was genuine. It was real. In fact, before I knew it we were yucking it up, each one of us catching the others laughter and both of us starting back up again.

As the laughter subsided, I spoke. "I never heard anyone call the Father the man upstairs."

"Really?"

"Really! Besides, when I feel and sometimes see the Father he's right here on the first floor."

"So you've seen the Father?" Miller asked, more than a little wary that he was probably dealing with a religious fanatic.

"Only on horseback," was my response.

"You mean the Father was on a horse, or you're on a horse?"

"Both."

There was a pause in the conversation as both he and I digested what had just been said. The breeze which had died down kicked up again. It felt good.

"When I was getting a drink and you and your horse rode up without making noise I thought you might be the Father."

"You thought a colored man might be God?"

"Why not?"

"No reason, but you know most colored people love Jesus who isn't colored."

"Yeah, I know. That's kind of weird, isn't it?"

Miller thought about that for a moment.

"You're right, son, it is weird."

"Mister, I like you. What's your name?"

"Lawrence Miller and please don't call me Larry." Miller told me his real name right off the bat. Now that ought to be worth something. It sure was to me.

"I'm John Wilson Barnes," I extended my open hand to Miller. Miller reached across his saddle and shook my hand.

"Mighty pleased to meet you, John," Miller said.

"Pleasure's mine and you don't have to worry about me calling you any nicknames. I'll always call you, Mr. Miller," I said continuing to shake Miller's hand.

By the time we'd finished shaking hands the horses had stopped. There was a huge moment of silence between us. A silence which neither of us had ever known. The silence full of peace happening when two souls burn together and like the burning.

"You'd better go back, John," Miller advised.

"I can ride on with you."

"I don't want to take you too far out of your way," Miller said.

"OK," I admitted, "I'll go back."

"You'll see me again, John."

"I will?"

"You will, and when you do, don't run from me."

"Why would I do that?"

"Just remember, don't run. Come to me. I can keep you safe."

I didn't know what to say. I understood Mr. Miller's words, and I almost grasped Miller's intention, but the time just wasn't ripe.

"Adios, Amigo," I whispered.

"Via con Padre," Miller said hoping I'd catch his meaning.

I knew *via con dios* meant *go with God.* And I knew the word Padre, I'd heard it before from some of the Mexican kids at Rock Ranch. Oh yeah, it meant Father. What Mr. Miller had said to me in Spanish was, *Go with the Father.*

I spun in my saddle to acknowledge Miller's advice, but when I turned Miller was nowhere to be seen. I looked left and right, behind and in front. It was like Mr. Miller had vanished. The thought occurred to me—maybe he had disappeared! Maybe, just maybe, my first inclination had been right. Perhaps, Mr. Miller was the Cowboy or the Father in disguise?

I knew I had to get back to Fort Apocalypse. And right now! The afternoon ride and the conversation with Mr. Miller/the Father/the Cowboy had been wonderful.

60

I loved working with the horses. I felt on some level that's what I was meant to do in life. And yet, the atmosphere around Fort Apocalypse was just plain weird.

When Arthur Bannack was away, everyone acted differently. They talked more, they were friendlier, and everything around the fort breathed a sigh of relief when Arthur Bannack drove off in his black Ford F-250. I didn't ever want Mr. Bannack to think I was ungrateful. I'd been taken into their group like the story in the Bible with the son who wanted his inheritance, got it, spent it, then came back home. The boy thought the father would hate him, but the earthly father, like our heavenly Father, only wanted the best for him. But, in the end, we must choose the best for ourselves.

I was the prodigal son of Fort Apocalypse. I knew I was the favorite son, but I suspected, just as in the biblical story, there were those who resented my rise to power and the favoritism.

Off a ways and traveling a different ridgeline, Agent Miller of Alcohol, Tobacco and Firearms' fame looked down upon me as I rode north. I wasn't sure why, but I thought Miller liked me. Heck, I think I even knew he was someone I should have avoided, and probably that he was following me now.

He told me later when things had settled down how he'd tried with his beloved wife, Sarah Rae, to make a family of his own. Yet, the two graves on his property in the Bitterroot Valley just south the Darby were dead proof he had failed. Once they'd gotten married, his wife wanted children. Careful what you ask for, you just might get it. The labor had come in the middle of the night. There was no time for anything but delivering the baby and in the awful, bloody process, both had died. That had been nearly fifteen years ago and somehow me, a long string of spit, young cowboy had reminded him of someone he'd never really know—his own dead infant son.

I came riding up as Arthur made his way across the compound and paddock area to the stables.

"Where you've been?"

"Just out."

"What'd you go out for?"

"These new horses have to be ridden if they're going to be any good."

"Makes sense," Arthur said, then added, "You didn't see any signs of people about, did you?"

"No," I lied, "just trees, hills, and sky. Beautiful day."

Arthur opened the gate and I rode on into the paddock area.

"I want you to keep as many horses that are rideable saddled and ready to go twenty-four seven."

"I'll need more tack."

"I've taken care of that. In the long horse trailer you'll find everything you'll need, saddles, head stalls, bits—everything you'll need."

"Are we expecting company?"

Arthur looked toward the closest mountains as if looking for intruders.

"I'm afraid so."

"Maybe you should send some sentries out?"

"That's not a bad idea."

"I'll saddle up some ponies for the sentries."

"Get some help and saddle as many of the horses that are rideable. I'll send six men down this way, have their horses ready." Arthur walked back toward the compound. I was sure glad scouts had not been put out earlier. They might have spotted Mr. Miller.

Edward Lee Bannack came down, and a few others who knew horses also came with him. The six scout horses were saddled first. Those men showed up with bedrolls and rations. I guessed they'd be stationed out on point for some time.

As the six rode out off in different directions, Ed turned to me as he threw a saddle on a horse.

"It's just about over here, ain't it, boy?"

"You think?"

"My son, Arthur, is sending out scouts. Bertha spilled her guts at the hospital." He paused, looked away then spoke again. "There's a secret hideout."

"Where's that?"

"Can't tell you without checking with my boy, but it ain't close. Maybe a week's ride on horseback if we have to stay hidden."

"How will I be able to find it?" I asked, actually concerned now for my own safety. If the law caught up with Bannack, they'd also catch up with me, John Wilson Barnes. I didn't relish spending the rest of my life in jail for the murder of that man whose name I will never mention again.

"Don't you worry, boy. You and I are the best horsemen here. You just stick to my tail and when the shit hits the fan, you'll be fine."

We saddled nearly fifty horses. The cinches were left loose and the head stalls were hanging off the saddle horns. When the time came they would be ready.

From my bunk bed I heard what I thought was someone's radio turned up way too loud. I roused myself, pulled on my jeans and boots and walked out of the tack-bedroom. Before I could get to the open end of the barn, Edward Lee Bannack came rushing in.

"Tighten the cinches and put on all the head stalls. The *shite's* about to hit the fan!"

Ed ran to the end of the barn and started in on the last horse.

I continued on out to the barn door. Once outside I just stood there, incredulous.

People were running helter-skelter and it didn't seem like they were doing anything which had any purpose. From the entrance of the barn I could hear Edward Lee Bannack placing head stalls on horses and tightening cinches. I couldn't hear the actual work as much as I heard the horses, some of them protesting the bit in their mouths.

The announcement came over the loudspeakers in the mountains.

"Attention to the fort below; in twenty-eight minutes a full assault on the fort will begin. Federal agents are here to remove you from protected federal lands and disarm you. Any attempt to resist their federally sanctioned warrants will be met with deadly force. All men, women and children who wish to surrender will proceed directly south where they will be welcomed by federal agents. You now have twenty-seven minutes to respond."

From his quarters, Arthur Bannack walked majestically toward the center of the parade grounds. His walk could be considered nothing but majestic because he seemed to be moving in slow motion while all those around him were doing double-time. Really, the only two people who weren't rushing around like chickens with their heads cut off were Arthur and me.

When he reached the platform he walked up the three steps and centered himself. He then raised the bullhorn which he was carrying at his side.

"Hey John," yelled Ed Bannack from inside the barn, "you want to help me with these horses?!"

I turned to reply as Bertha Lynn Bannack ran past me. She ran to her husband, Ed, and began placing head stalls on horses and tightening cinches.

I wanted to help them. I really did. But there was something about the scene swirling around me which kept me glued to the spot I was standing on.

214

Arthur Bannack slowly raised the bullhorn to his mouth.

"Brothers and sisters," he began in a slow, even cadence. "Today is the day we have all been waiting for. Fort Apocalypse will now fulfill its name."

Many of those who had been scurrying around with no purpose stopped in front of the raised platform. Bannack continued.

"Law enforcement doesn't give a rat's ass about your safety. Those who choose to surrender will be manacled and put in cages. Their children will be separated from them and they will never see their progeny again."

Some of those who had gathered certain possessions and their children and had started toward the southern surrender spot stopped, turned, and listened.

"This fort has been your home now for quite a while. The mud races want your white children so they can intermarry with them and make them parents of other mud people. The mud people will stop at nothing to destroy your perfect DNA."

Many of those who had walked quite a ways south, turned and walked back toward the fort.

Arthur Bannack smiled. I saw now, the fear of their imminent deaths was nothing compared to their fear of the intermarriage of their children. When you have a megalomaniac with low self-esteem, you have a leader who is willing to sacrifice everything for the cause. All one has to do is remember Hitler and the last days of the thousand year Reich in a ruined and bombed out Berlin.

"What needs to happen now," Bannack said over the bullhorn, "is for us to stand up to these murderous bastards. They only have a job to do today: They want to kill us! We have so much more! We have a cause! This may be the finest hour of the Caucasian race. If we are victorious we will be remembered down through history until the end of time. If the government SOBs win it will also be remembered as the most tragic hour in the history of mankind. They will stand atop the mounds of our dead. They will take pictures to prove their victory. But our bodies, torn and mutilated, the bodies of our innocent white children raped and beheaded, will speak louder than their victorious smiles."

I'd never heard anything as ridiculous and mean-spirited as that speech. I knew, I knew it wasn't true, yet those who had begun to surrender, to leave and save their lives and the lives of their children had now turned around and were coming back toward the fort across open ground.

I stood frozen at the entrance of the barn. I felt like surrendering, but was sure Arthur Bannack would shoot me dead if I made a move in that direction.

Bertha and Ed were nearly a third of the way done with the head stalls and tightening the cinches.

I had made sure neither Tia nor China had been saddled. Now, I was more worried about my two horses. Well, actually Tia was mine and China was my best friend's horse. I was worried they would be killed in the coming battle. I had to get them out of harm's way.

As I turned to go back to the barn a new wrinkle was sent forth by the government men. A Huey helicopter—fully equipped with 50 caliber machine guns —flew in low from the South.

The people who had been surrendering and now were hurrying back to the fort picked up their children and ran even faster when they heard the rotary wings of the Huey slashing through the early morning mist.

The helicopter had had the effect the government wanted. It certainly wasn't shock and awe, but it was a major form of intimidation.

Later I learned Lawrence Miller, Senior ATF agent in charge watched with his binoculars from the Eastern Mountains. He was sitting atop Beaute and with the rising sun behind him, he was virtually invisible to anyone at the fort.

Miller scanned once again past the panicked multitudes,

some of whom were simply running in circles. He found his target about the same time his target had found another target.

Arthur Bannack raised the bazooka to his shoulder and judged the shot on the approaching Huey. The missile streaked an ugly smoky line from Bannack's shoulder to the underbelly of the Huey.

The fully-armed helicopter blew up and rained down destruction upon those returning to the fort. Men, women, and children were on fire and running to their deaths. Those not consumed by fire were blown to bits as the armed ordinance skipped and danced across the valley floor before unleashing their catastrophic explosions. When the smoke cleared the southern field was strewn with the bodies of burned, dead, and dying souls.

Miller almost did a double take as Bannack could be seen through the binocs. Bannack was laughing hysterically and doing a jig on the raised platform. Miller had seen the same dance, the same maniacal expression on film when Poland had fallen in 1938 and Hitler had danced the jig in victory.

Frantically, Agent Miller moved the binoculars. Arthur Bannack was nowhere to be seen. Agent Miller had lost track of him. There were burning people and exploding ordinances. There were men setting up 60 caliber machine guns, women running around looking for their children, children standing alone, their mouths agape in what looked to Miller to be silent screams.

Then, he saw the man of the drover's coat. He was mounted on a bay horse and came exploding from the barn.

I turned when I heard the sound of pounding hooves. Bannack didn't slow down. I barely had time to jump out of the way before Bannack ran me down on the bay.

I picked myself up off the ground. Arthur Bannack, the man who had taken me in and told everyone I was the answer to their prayers, that same man had nearly run me over. And it wasn't an accident! Arthur Bannack had ridden the horse directly at me.

I figured it was time to either cut bait or fish. Fort

Apocalypse was falling down around everyone's ears. It was time for me to take care of my business.

Inside the barn, way in the back, I had saddled the horse I'd arrived on—the one I'd stolen from Rock Ranch. Behind that Roan was Tia and China. They had halters on and their lead ropes were tied to one of the stalls. I had suspected this might happen and I'd prepared beforehand. In the middle of all this confusion, I planned to take my three horses and leave. I tied China's lead to Tia's tail and after untying Tia, I mounted the Roan.

"Where you going, boy?" Bertha said as she pointed Ed's old pistol at me. I could see the jacketed rounds winking at me from the exposed cylinders of the large weapon.

"It's time to leave."

"Well, we're not through saddling these mounts for the leadership," Bertha spat out.

"The leadership just took the first horse he could find and nearly killed me as he hightailed it out a here."

"He's going to the hideout. Where are you going?"

"Bertha Lynn, what are you doing?" Edward Lee Bannack stood behind his wife and to the side. His hands were behind his back.

"This boy's about to leave all the work to us," Bertha said without turning around.

"Let the boy go, Bertha, he never did anything to us."

"No!" Bertha shouted, "Someone has to show some balls around here!"

Ed swung the 2 x 4 quickly and skillfully. Bertha went down like a snowman in August.

"Go on, boy," Ed said, then smiled at me.

I wasted no time as I rode the Roan around Bertha's body. Tia and China followed, carefully stepping around the downed woman's body.

"Thanks, Ed," I shouted as I rode from the relative quiet of the barn out into the chaos surrounding Fort Apocalypse.

61

I rode away toward the mountains bordering on the east. I could hear the ratta-tat-tat of automatic weapons fire. Bullets whizzed past me and my three horses. I said a quick prayer that the four of us would make it to the woods before we were killed or wounded.

Making the woods, I stopped and inspected the three horses. None of them had been hit, none of them were wounded. I mounted the Roan again before starting off I bowed my head and said a prayer.

"Cowboy," I began, "I know I've done a lot of bad things. I also know that you've forgiven me. Now, all four of us want your protection. I don't know where I'm going or how I'm going to get there. But I know you know. Guide me, let me hear your voice in the voices of others; let me see your face in the faces of others. But mostly let me die before any of these innocent horses are harmed."

I opened my eyes half expecting to see the Cowboy sitting on his magnificent steed as I had seen Him as a child. Instead, the sun broke through the clouds and lit up a path through the woods and up the mountain.

"Thank you," I whispered as I tickled the Roan's side with my spurs.

I rode up the trail to the eastern mountains. I was going to make my escape. I would find somewhere to hide until this all blew over, that's what I was telling myself as I rounded a bend in the trail.

"Federal Agent, put your hands in the air!" Miller recited. My Roan was startled by the large black horse. The Roan reared up and I tumbled to the ground.

"What the—" Miller began as another horse and rider rode up behind him. Bannack had expected federal agents to be in the hills east of the fort, but he had never, ever expected a black agent!

"Throw your weapon down, or I'll kill the boy," Bannack spat out.

Arthur Bannack's cocked pistol was pointed at me as I lay on the ground.

Miller thought about just shooting the drover coat man and letting the chips fall where they may, but deep inside him—even more than not shedding innocent horse blood—Miller didn't want the blood of the innocent boy shed.

Miller dropped the Army 45 automatic.

"Now, the holstered weapon on your side," Bannack barked.

Miller slipped the .44 mag single action pistol from his holster and let it, too, drop to the ground.

"John-boy," Bannack said. "Hey, that sounds so homey, like we're in the South fighting the Civil War. John-boy, since you're already on the ground, pick up the agent's pistolas."

I picked them up one by one and butt end first handed them out to Bannack.

"No, John-boy, no," Bannack began, "I've been wanting to get this part of your initiation done for some time now. You take the pistolas and fill the agent here with holes."

I reversed the backwards pistols in my hands—I'd learned that trick from the cowboy movies. I looked at Agent Miller whom I knew didn't have one evil bone in his body, then I looked at Bannack, perhaps, the most evil person I'd ever known. I could still see the Huey pin wheeling down in flames upon the men, women, and children whom Bannack had begged to come back to the fort. I thought about the Father and the cup he'd offered the Savior in the Garden of Gethsemane. I wondered if this was to be my cup, the one I couldn't pass on or pass up.

"John-boy, you aren't exactly doing what I want. But then again maybe you never killed a man before, being of such a young and tender age. Maybe you need some encouragement," Bannack said as he swung his gun from covering the agent to pointing directly at me.

"Oh, I killed a man once. Didn't mean to, but that didn't make him any less dead," I said.

I pulled back the hammer on the single action .44 mag and pointed it at Miller. "Do you have anything to say, sir, before I blow you into tomorrow?"

Bannack loved this kind of sick shit. He was grinning from ear to ear. Miller looked directly at me.

"The Lord giveth, the Lord taketh away," Miller recited from memory.

"Blessed be the name of the Lord," I said, as I flicked the Army 45 in Miller's direction and fanned the hammer on the .44 three times.

Lucky, or was it blessed? The first shot tore a hole in Bannack's right shoulder and the gun he had aimed at me fell free from his grip. The second shot gave him a low part over his left ear stinging like mad. The third shot entered his lower abdomen and ripped through Bannack's half-digested breakfast. Bannack threw up blood, then fell from his horse head first.

The entire town of East Glacier Park had become a triage unit for war victims. Medics were airlifted in to take care of the wounded, and coroner's vans from one hundred miles away picked up the casualties. The town resembled the behind the lines staging area for a major battle in a major war.

Those who could not be helped were given morphine and attended to by the ministers of the town. There was even a vacationing Rabbi who went about blessing the dead and offering solace to the wounded.

Bannack had been airlifted to the East Glacier Park Hospital and was halfway through an eight hour surgery. He was expected to live, but also expected to lose a good six feet of intestines.

I sat in the front of Agent Miller's car, a pair of handcuffs attached to me and the passenger door. They were afraid I might run. I was positive my running days were through.

Miller came from the hospital. His head was down against a north wind. He got in the car and reached for the ignition key. Before he turned the key, he turned to me.

"He'll live," was all Miller said before he cranked the engine over.

We backed from the parking space and left the hospital parking lot.

"Are you taking me to jail?" I asked, sure I was headed in that direction.

"Nah," Miller began, "we're going to pick up my truck."

We drove to the outskirts of town, where Miller's Dodge

pickup was parked with a fine horse trailer attached to it. I was sure I saw Tia's head through the high windows in the trailer.

"Is that one of my horses in your trailer?"

Miller reached over me and unlocked the cuffs, then he got out of the car. I got out and looked over the top of the car at Miller.

"No," Miller said, "it wasn't one of your horses you saw. It was one of my horses and three of your horses."

I skipped over to the back of the trailer and looked in.

"Tia, China, Roan-boy," I nearly shouted.

Tia answered with a low chortle that sounded like a souped-up V-8 in a 1950s Ford pickup.

Miller got in the truck and started the diesel engine up. It rumbled to life.

I tried to open the passenger door of the truck, but it was locked. Me and Miller looked at each other through the glass. Miller smiled and pulled the lock up on the door.

As we drove out of East Glacier Park I turned to Miller.

"Where are we going?"

"Have you ever been to the Bitterroot Valley?"

Things which are meant to be will be, no matter how much or hard you try to stop them. Things which are not meant to be will never be, no matter how hard or much you try to make them happen.

From the moment Agent Lawrence Miller had seen me, he knew, Agent Miller did, he knew he and I were connected and the connection had come from the Father.

And then what? He fought the desire to help me. But if it was from the Father, how could he fight it?

All of the Roman Empire had stood up against the Father's Son. They had imprisoned him, scourged him, spit on him and tortured him to death on the cross. But Father uses the might and wisdom of the world to show the world how wrong it can be. After they had placed the Father's Son in a tomb and surrounded it with Rome's finest, even after all that, on the morning of the third day the Son walked from his tomb, from his death. Quite frankly, the world had never, ever been the same again.

So what good would it do a senior Negro ATF Agent to deny what God, the Father, had ordained?

We rode to Rock Ranch. I was sitting in Miller's truck when the man whose name I will never mention was handcuffed and walked out to a Montana State Trooper's cruiser. He was to stand trial for the drugging and rape of many young boys. Once the news had spread, twenty-five young men came forward to testify. The trial was short, but the sentence was long: Life in prison with no chance of parole. Montana would put up with lots of things, but pedophiles weren't one of them!

For me the sentencing had been much more satisfying than if he would have died. The best part was the man whose name I will never mention still wore the dent and scar in his head from Tia's hoof.

Agent Miller had me return the Roan to Rock Ranch. It had served me well and come to no harm.

Tia and China were purchased by Miller and when I profusely thanked him for doing so, Miller simply reminded me I'd be doing chores at Miller's ranch to pay him back.

A long and exhaustive search was made for Edward Lee Bannack and his wife, Bertha. Many had been captured, many killed at Fort Apocalypse, but neither of those two were ever seen again.

When Miller's truck drove onto his three hundred acres outside Darby, Tia, China, and Beaute were in the horse trailer behind it.

I saw the modest house and outbuildings, but right before we got to these buildings Miller made a left turn up a dirt road which ascended into the surrounding hills. At the edge of the forest a giant oak grew. Beneath it there were two headstones.

Miller stopped the truck and got out. The horses whinnied as if they wanted out, too. Miller walked to the headstones and stopped. I walked up and stood beside him.

Miller's head was bowed in prayer. I bowed my head, also. We stood there for a while. I wished Father/Cowboy on his magnificent steed would show up and I half expected to see Him when I looked up. It certainly felt like he was there.

Instead, I saw Miller's profile in the afternoon sun blazing through the clouds forming what looked like a halo encircling Miller's head.

One word escaped my lips. I said it softly and with great reverence.

"Father."

Miller opened his eyes and turned to look at the boy the

state of Montana had allowed him to adopt.

The light on my face was fresh and had a glow to it.

"Son," Miller said.

Miller and I embraced on that hillside. Our hug ended with the back pounding men are prone to do when words fail them.

And from that moment on, we both understood. The Father and the Son are best seen in their truest form, and their most endearing manner, in the faces of those we decide to love.

COMING SOON:
GRASS CREEK
THE SEQUEL TO BITTERROOT VALLEY

Prologue
Cheyenne Memorial Hospital

When I looked up, Mariah was weeping softly. I'd finished the part of my story which she didn't know. I'd brought her from the loss of my parents to the gaining of my new father, Agent Lawrence Miller. I'd told her about how I'd been found guilty of horse thievery and the consequences of such things. I'd even told her about the man whose name I will never speak again, and to tell the truth, not anybody but Cheyenne and Dwight ever knew that story. I'm not even sure if Dwight told Yolanda or not. Didn't matter now, Dwight and Cheyenne were both dead, and the story had died with them. It was good to tell at least one other soul and a blood relation at that. Something about telling Mariah the story had lifted a weight off my chest. I'd gotten rid of something which I no longer wished to carry. She was still crying.

"I didn't mean to upset you, darlin'."

She reached out and took my hand in both of hers and buried her wet face on top of it.

"It's the most wonderful story I've ever heard, Papa, ever!" She said this into my hand and then she lifted her face and smiled a big smile, the way the young are able to do, automatically switching from sorrow to joy.

"There's more, isn't there?"

"You knew your great granddaddy; you were around for some time before he passed on."

"But what about the time you spent living on the ranch outside Darby?"

"Those were wonderful years. I even kept a journal of sorts. You ever notice it's ladies that keep diaries and men always call 'em journals?"

"Tell me about those years."

"I will. Why don't you come back tomorrow and bring that boy friend of yours along."

"Really? That would be wonderful. I think he deserves to hear just as much as I do."

"I agree. You run along, and when you come back tomorrow, I'll tell both of you about it."

And that's what I intended to do, but as everyone knows, the road to hell and all that. The next morning, when Mariah arrived with her boyfriend in tow, the room I'd been in was empty. Once again she broke down into tears and thought I'd died in the night.

She wasn't far from the truth. I did have a heart attack, and without modern medicine I would have been a goner, but they brought me back. All of this was explained to Mariah by one of my nurses. She and her beau rushed down to ICU, but all they could do was look at me through a picture window. 'Fraid I didn't make much of an impression, hooked up like I was. I looked more like a rocket getting ready to launch into space than a man. So many tubes running here and there, and in and out. It was a good ten days before I was back in my regular room.

They were sitting in the comfortable chairs and sipping on a Pepsi with lots of ice when I opened my eyes.

"Papa, do you know who I am?"

"Is this a trick question?"

She turned to her beau and gave his hand a squeeze.

"He knows."

"Hey, Mr. Barnes. You feelin' OK?"

"Boy, don't ever ask a man who just about died if he's feelin' OK. I feel like hammered buffalo chips, that's how I feel."

Mariah scooted a bit closer, keeping her beau's hand in hers.

"He's got a couple of days off, why don't you tell us about the time you spent on the ranch in the Bitterroot with Great Grandpa Miller."

"There's a journal where you can read about all that. With this new weakness I think I'd better get on and tell you about the last part; when I met your grandma and such."

"But I know most of that!" she protested.

"Bet you didn't know your great grandpa Miller was murdered before I even met your grandmother?"

"But how—"

"You two just sit back and let me tell you both just how it shook out."

CPSIA information can be obtained
at www.ICGtesting.com
Printed in the USA
LVOW13s2248200218
567275LV00014B/1393/P